All is Bright - A Yorkshire Lad's Christmas
By Dave Preston

I0631050

All is Bright - A Yorkshire Lad's Christmas

Dave Preston

Published by Dave Preston, 2025.

For Lesley

---

1. https://www.collectionscanada.gc.ca/ciss-ssci/app/
index.php?fuseaction=logbook.edit&publication=537090&lang=eng

Also by Dave Preston

Yorkshire's Christmas Recipes (White Rose Content)

The Story of Butchart Gardens (Highline Publishing)
Rails & Rooms – A Timeless Canadian Journey
(Whitecap Books)
It's Time I Told You [Poetry] (White Rose Content)

Try and Stop Me! [Poetry] (White Rose Content)

Waiting for Godonlyknows [Play] (White Rose Content)

Take Three [Play] (White Rose Content)

Personals [Play] (White Rose Content)

Dave Preston also contributed to the following books:
Northwest Best Places
Idiot's Guide to Canada in the 60s, 70s, & 80s
The Canadian Book of Lists

Foreward

I've always loved Christmas, and the older I get the more I enjoy the season. However, as much as I look forward to the next 24th of December, I find myself looking back quite fondly at all the Christmases I've been fortunate enough to have, especially those I enjoyed as a child.

It didn't seem to be so much about stuff, back then. Even though the untidy letters I sent up the chimney to Father Christmas were a bit lengthy and bordering on greed, asking for more than I really deserved or realistically expected. Just because my mother so often said "We can't afford it" didn't mean that Father Christmas couldn't afford it. They were simple times, and occasionally lean times by today's standards, but looking back through the rosey hindsight of nostalgia, they were good, often magical times, and times I feel are worth re-visiting.

Of course, Christmas is a lovely occasion to celebrate, to relax the reins of restraint and enjoy the fruits of our year's labour with good food and drink. But today's Christmas, plagued by crass commercialism and over indulgence, even entitlement, risks becoming fat, bloated, and hollow, as opposed to fat, jolly, and full of fun.

I recall a time when most Christmas shopping was done just a week or two before, and almost everyone worked right up to the afternoon of Christmas Eve. The holiday lasted for just two well-filled days, for most of us. (Those of us on farms worked with the animals just like we did on every other day.)

Now we're encouraged to start shopping months before, and keep on shopping well into January. I must confess that I find it hard to hold off on pulling out all the lights and decorations until December, but I do.

These stories are largely fiction, but there's a dose of truth in every one of them. Ten-year-old Derek Bradley and his younger brother, Jimmy, didn't really exist, or maybe they did. Maybe they lived in every little Yorkshire village. The settings for the stories are real enough, and readers familiar with the village of Old Malton and the market town of Malton, just up the road, might recognise a few of the places and some of the characters.

I hope you try a few of the traditional Bradley-style Christmas recipes that appear towards the end of the book, and that you generously fill your season with well-fed good company. I also hope you enjoy this collection of festive tales that were born in the years when, as Derek would say, "Christmas was real, and fun, and real funny." Some might say we don't make them like that anymore, but I think we can if we try.

Dave Preston

The Stories

In no particular order

1

The Christmas Kiss

Me and me Dad were in the kitchen, untangling the Christmas lights for the tree, not that we had one yet. We always waited until just before Christmas cos Dad said that's when they got cheap.

"Hey, you'll never guess what the carol singers from the church made the other night," said Mam as she came in.

"No," he said.

"Go on, guess," said Mam.

"Ten quid," said Dad.

"Twenty-seven pounds!" me Mam said. "*Twenty-seven pounds!*"

"Twenty-seven quid! And they were only out for an hour weren't they?"

"Yes," said Mam, "Mind there was a good turnout, the full choir."

It got me thinking did that. Twenty-seven pounds just for singing a few Christmas songs. I could sing.

By the time I went to bed the plan was just about made. I'd go carol singing the next night, and make a fortune. But I didn't like the idea of going by meself. I'd need a mate, someone who could sing, someone who could walk round the village at night, and most of all, someone who could keep quiet about it.

Most of the kids at our school came in on a bus, from the farms roundabout. There were only twelve kids lived in the village itself. When you took away the infants and all the kids younger than me, and the five who were up at the big school, there was only one left. Josie Carter. A girl! Mind, she could sing. But I couldn't go round with a girl. Never. I couldn't get to sleep. I had to go carol singing, I just had to...

Next day at school I kept looking round at all the kids in our class. When we sang the morning hymn I listened to 'em all. Most of 'em sounded alright, but that was only when we all sang together. If Mrs Heath ever wanted just one person to sing, she either asked me, or... yeah, Josie Carter.

It had to be her. Or nobody, and I wasn't going to let all this money go as easy as that. I'd have to ask her at playtime, in secret. We were larkin' football and I kicked the ball across to her, and when I went to get it back, I leaned over and whispered. I want a word.

"Yeah?" she said.

Shh, I said, no not here, after school, at shop corner, right?

"Alright," she said, and I kicked the ball back to me mates.

After school she was waiting for me just around the corner from the shop. Now then, I said, do you want to make some easy money?

"I'm not showing you me knickers," she said.

No, not that, I mean carol singing.

She said "Carol singing?"

Yeah, you and me, tonight.

"Where?"

Here. Round t'village.

"Ooh, I don't know about that," she said, "I think I'd rather show you me knickers."

Aw, come on, I said, it'll be a doddle. And think of the money! That church lot made twenty-seven quid!

"Oh, alright then, come for me at seven o'clock."

No, I'll meet you back here.

"Alright then, see ya" and she skipped off up Westgate, singing *O Come All Ye Faithful*.

I could hardly eat me tea I was that excited. I never said a word about it to anybody, I just said I had to go out later and see a mate about summat. At five to seven I went back to the shop corner and Josie was waiting. It was a cold night, bit foggy, and she was all wrapped up with a scarf and gloves, as well as her duffle coat. Now then, I said, let's start at the other end, and we walked up the village to Cottage Row.

"Righto, shall we knock and then start singing?"

No! I said, we'll sing first, then knock. And you'll have to take that scarf off your face else they won't hear ya.

"But what if they're watching telly? They won't hear us and when we knock they'll want another song."

No, I said, it's best if we just sing. Loud. They'll stop what they're doing and listen, (I'd seen this happen in a film once). Then we knock and wish 'em Merry Christmas and they give us money. Easy.

"Alright then," she said. I liked Josie, cos she never argued for long.

See, what Josie didn't realise was that as soon as we knocked on the door, I was going to bugger off round the nearest corner, leaving her to get to the money. I wanted it to snow cos that makes people feel more Christmassy and they'd give us more money. But it was foggy instead, which was alright cos it was easier to hide in.

First door we tried there was nobody in, even though there was a light on. Then we went next door and Mrs Dobson gave us threepence for two verses of Good King Wenceslas. This was going to be easy.

We soon had the routine down - we'd sing two verses, Josie would knock and I'd bugger off. Then she'd come and find me and tell me what we'd been given. Nobody seemed to notice there was two voices singing but only one person at the door. Mrs Bradshaw said she hadn't got any change and gave Josie an orange instead. It was getting colder but we kept going and by eight o'clock we'd done all the houses we wanted to. A lot of people seemed to be out, even though their telly was on.

Had enough? I said, as we got to the corner of Westgate.

"Yeah, and I'm a bit cold," she said, "Can I put me scarf back on?" She'd had to take her gloves off anorl, so people could hear her knocking on the door. Alright, let's go to your lane end and sort out what we've got. We pulled out all the coins and put 'em on the wall and started counting. We had one and six between us.

"Don't forget the orange," said Josie, holding it up like it was the FA cup. Oh aye, I said, but I don't like oranges, you can have it.

"Ta," she said. Then I suddenly realized the bloomin' orange was part of our earnings. Hey, that orange, how much is it worth?

"Oh, I don't know," she said, "Me mam always buys at least six. I think she pays about two bob." I started doing the sums in me head...

"Fourpence," she said. Is it? I said. Are you sure? Fourpence apiece? Right then, so if that orange is worth fourpence, and we add that to the one and six, we get, er...

"One and ten," she said. Right, one and ten, between the two of us that makes, er...

"Eleven pence each," she said.

Alright then, eleven pence each. Hang on, it doesn't work, I said. It won't go, we haven't got enough pennies. I suddenly had an idea. Hey that's a bloomin' big orange, I said. I bet you wouldn't get six oranges *that* size for two bob. I'd bet you'd only get, ooh, maybe four.

"You mean sixpence each?" Aye, I said. So, if you keep that orange I'll have the tanner we've got here and we're all even, right, and I shoved the two threepenny bits in her coat pocket and put the rest of the cash in mine. Right, I said, that's that. I'll be off then.

"Yeah," she said, "It was a laugh eh?" Yeah, maybe we'll do it again next year. See ya, and I turned to go.

"Hey Derek?" she says, Yeah? I said, and when I turned back she was right in front of me, smiling at me and taking her scarf off.

"What about a Christmas kiss then?"

You what? I said.

"Go on Derek, it's nearly Christmas. Linda Smith says you like me, and I know you won't give me one at school." Damn right I won't I thought to meself. Then I had a clever thought, Aw, sorry I said, I've got no mistletoe. Kuh!

"We don't need mistletoe, that's just for old folks, come here." And she grabbed the front of me duffle coat and pulled me right up to herself. I didn't know what to do.

She was the same height as me, and her nose was really close. I could feel her breath. Then she closed her eyes, really slow, and her lips kind of squished up together and reached out, all on their own, towards me.

I couldn't move. Everything went quiet. I stopped breathing. She stopped breathing. Everything stopped, I think the street light might have gone out cos it suddenly seemed to go all dark and then before I knew what was happening...

I was doing it. Giving her a kiss. Me! *Kissing!* I was kissing Josie Carter! In public, right there at the bottom of Suggett's Lane! Kissing... on the mouth, and... and... and by gum it felt good. Lovely.

It weren't like a kiss from me Mam, or me aunt Judy, or like any other kiss I'd ever had. It was bloomin' great. Nice. Soft. Warm. Better than toffee, better than chocolate, even better than Turkish Delight. I closed me eyes anorl. Me and Josie were kissing...

Oh... goodness me... bloody hell... Then she stopped and took her lips away. I opened me eyes and I could feel the cold air on me face again. It stopped being nice.

"Goodnight!" she said, and she turned and ran up the lane towards her house.

I felt a bit dizzy, and suddenly remembered I had to breathe so I sucked in a great big lungful, then blew it all back into the night... you could see it go up into the air, like smoke from a gun. I turned and ran anorl, all the way back home, with streetlights twinkling and the money jangling in me pocket.

I was still a bit dizzy when I walked into the house. They were all in the front room, and me Dad was still on the floor wrestling with the Christmas lights and quietly saying bad words. He didn't look happy.

"There you are, Derek, where've you been?" Mam shouted, "Come and see yer Aunt Hilda. Be sharp, she's leaving in a minute."

She must have come to bring the Christmas presents I thought, so I took me coat and wellies off. Me Aunt Hilda was a big woman, real big, and strong. Dad said she could lift a bag o'coal up with one hand and carry the shovel in the other. I'd never seen her do it but I'd like to.

Aunt Hilda hadn't got married so there wasn't an uncle there, and she lived all on her own at the edge of the moors. Some kids in our village said she was a witch, but she wasn't really. She never wore a pointy hat like they do. And she had the wrong hair, it was all white. She would have made a good Mrs for Father Christmas cos she had white whiskers anorl. Thick, curly ones on her top lip and all over her chin, but you weren't supposed to say anything about 'em. As soon as I got near she grabbed hold o'me.

"Now then young Derek," she said, pulling me in and crushing me up against her stomach, "Say hello to your old aunt Hilda! Would you like a Christmas kiss?"

No thank-you, I said, I've just had one.

2

Paradise Lost

It was Friday, the week before Christmas, the day before Christmas shopping day. Pay day for me Dad, and funny thing was, he was late home from work. It was bangers and mash for tea, like every Friday, and Dad wouldn't be late for that.

Me and our Jimmy were watching for him from the front room window. It was real cold outside, and there was snow, but we had a big fire on. The steam from the clothes horse kept fogging up the glass, so I kept having to wipe it with Jimmy's sleeve.

Me Dad was never late on Fridays, and me Mam didn't know where he was, but she knew he had a big pay packet this week, cos he's in the firm's Christmas club. This means that they save a bit out of his wages every week, all year, then he gets it all back on the week before Christmas, so's he can give it to Mam for the Christmas shopping. Shopping was tomorrow.

It was going to be great cos we'd get to have our dinners in the cafe and then go to the CO-OP and sit on Father Christmas' knee and tell him what we want. Then we'd even get a taxi back home cos we had too much stuff to carry. But that wasn't til tomorrow. That's the worst thing about Christmas, all this bloomin' waiting.

Anyway, it was well past five o'clock when we finally heard him open the front gate, and he was singing, which was daft cos me Dad can't sing. Then we heard him shout *ARGH!* and by the time we got to the window all we could see was his legs sticking out from under the big bush inside the gate. And his bike was on top of 'im. Me and Jimmy had spent all afternoon making a real good slide down the front path and I think he must have slipped on it.

So, he finally comes in through the back door and he's red in the face and rubbin' his leg, but still fairly happy. Him and Mam have a few quiet words while me and Jimmy are sent to wash our hands. Seems he'd been to the pub with his work mates, since it was Christmas, and he'd had a drink. Seems he'd had a few drinks, seen as it was Christmas, and I thought there was going to be

15

a war on cos Mam wiped her hands real hard on her pinny like she does just before we get a slap, but then Dad pulls a piece of mistletoe out of his pocket and holds it over her head, then winks at us and gives her a big kiss. She calmed down a bit after that and served up the tea, bangers and mash, my favourite.

We're all dying to talk about Christmas shopping, well, I am, but nobody says anything, until I ask what time we're going. "Early," says Mam, then she says to me Dad, "So, how much is there?" nodding to his jacket on the back of the chair.

"Oh, about forty quid," he says, real casual, as though he gets forty quid every week, instead of ten. "Ooh, no, hang on," he says, "I had a drink or two with the lads so maybe there's just thirty-odd."

"Good," says Mam, "cos it's already spent." I thought for a minute that we weren't going to get to go down Malton shopping next day, but then I remembered that she always says that when he gets paid.

"Right, let's have it then," she says and holds out her hand, which he kisses, what with him being still daft from the pub. Then he reaches into his jacket pocket, then into the other pocket, then he takes the jacket off the chair... and all the time his face is getting less and less happy. He finally stands up and goes through his trouser pockets, front and back, then he turns the jacket inside out... then he gets his lunch bag from off the kitchen door knob and goes through that, turning it upside down and dropping the flask out which lands on the floor and breaks inside, like they do. He sat down again. He looked a bit sad and a bit angry. He couldn't find it. He'd lost his big wage packet with all the Christmas money.

Mam had been walking up and down the kitchen, then came over to him. "How can you lose the Christmas wage packet?" she said, not very happy now and certainly not wanting another kiss under the mistletoe. Not that he was offering. Dad was looking real sad, and trying to think. He said he'd taken his jacket off in the pub cos it was warm and cos he was playing darts, and he left it hanging over a stool.

"Oh, I bet some rotten sod's pinched it," says Mam, also sounding quite sad now. Dad just looked down into his plate of mash and said nothing. Me and Jimmy knew to keep quiet so we did.

We went to bed early that night and heard Mam and Dad talking downstairs, quietly, with the telly turned off. Jimmy whispered across to me,

"It's a good thing Father Christmas brings the presents and we don't have to buy 'em, else it would be a bloomin' lean do this year."

Next day we were up early to get ready for shopping, but Mam said we needn't bother. She'd go on her own cos she hadn't got much money and she didn't want us nattering for stuff she couldn't afford. So me and Jimmy stayed home with me Dad. He said sorry to her as she left the house, and I think he must have said it lots of times last night cos she didn't seem to notice, and her eyes were all red.

When she'd gone Dad says "Right, lads, we'll put the decorations up," which we did, fairly quickly cos there weren't many. Every year we say we'll get more but we never do. The house still didn't look right.

"There's no tree!" said Jimmy.

"Aye, son, I know," said Dad, as if he did know but couldn't do anything about it, like when you tell him it's raining.

"Maybe we can go and find one cos Mam won't be bringing one back, she hasn't got enough money for that." No money for a tree? I thought that usually came top of the list but Dad said we needed food first and there wouldn't be much of that this year either. I could see he was still sad, but he was being what Granny would call a brave little soldier. Though he didn't look very brave right now. Mind, I've never seen him cry so I didn't think he'd start now.

Dad went out to the coalhouse and got his saw and me and Jimmy put our coats and wellies on. We went into the backyard and Dad said "Ey up, it looks like snow," and we said great but he didn't think so, and he went back in to get his cap. That's when he remembered that he'd lost his cap last night anorl. It must be in the pub with the wage packet. I said why not go back to the pub and ask but he said there was as much chance of his wage packet still being there as there was of our Jimmy sleeping in past ten o'clock on Christmas morning.

Dad needed a hat, though, so I said he could borrow my other one, the one Granny made me for last year. I went and got it and gave it to him. Our Jimmy looked as if to say Dad's not that daft, but he was, and he put it on. I hated that hat on me, but it looked great on Dad. It was that real scratchy wool, a funny grey colour and it had a big pom pom on top, which was lopsided and hung down the back of his head. He looked like a fat squirrel.

Anyway, we got set off up the backyard and over the fence into Cuppo's field.

"I know where we'll go," said Dad, "I know where there's a load o'nice Christmas trees to choose from," and he was looking towards the moors, towards the colonel's estate. Me and Jimmy knew we hadn't to go near there. Mam said we'd end up in prison if we ever went in there. But this was Dad's idea so we'd be alright.

Goin' over the fields Dad was still real quiet so I thought I'd cheer things up a bit with a Christmas song, but I didn't want to start on me own, and Jimmy wouldn't sing cos he was too busy whining about losing his socks off inside his wellies. "Come on," said Dad, "Keep up, we've a long way go to go. And keep yer eyes open." He never said what for.

I was freezing. It wasn't as much fun as shopping. Mam would be in Woolworths by now, where it was warm and smelled of baking and goodies. I was just looking at the fat squirrel bouncing around on Dad's head as he trudged us through hedges and over ditches, without ever stopping to have a rest or give us some chocolate, if he had any.

We finally got to a barbed wire fence with a lot of fir trees behind it, which we knew was the edge of the colonel's estate. There was a white sign with big red letters saying *Keep Out* cos he kept pheasants and stuff in there so him and his mates could shoot 'em.

"Alright," said Dad, in a quiet voice, looking up and down the fence, "You hold the wire down and me and Jimmy'll get through then we'll hold it down for you." so I did. It was like that film I saw a few weeks back, about some soldiers getting out of a prison camp in the war, but they were getting out of trouble and it seemed to me like we were struggling to get into it.

But then I thought if we did get caught it wouldn't be our fault cos Dad was there and they wouldn't report him to the police, I don't think. And besides, it was only fair cos we needed a Christmas tree and we'd lost our money. And there were loads of trees, the colonel wouldn't miss one.

Anyway, we were soon standing among the trees and Dad pointed to a good one, about six feet tall, dark green and real thick and bushy.

"Right," he said, "you lads keep a look out and I'll cut the bugger down." he doesn't usually say words like that in front of us so he must have been as excited as we were. He went round the other side, knelt down and was soon sawing away at the tree, while me and Jimmy kept a lookout, though Jimmy was still whining and asking me to take his wellies off and see to his socks.

"Good, just about there," said Dad, then it started to come down, right on top of me and Jimmy, and I shouted Ey up! But then there was a huge *BANG!* and twigs and fir needles were going in me eyes and Jimmy screamed.

"*Bloody hell fire!*" said Dad coming round to our side, "What the 'ell was that?" We all grabbed hold of each other, me and Dad hugging with Jimmy stuck in between us. Then we heard a voice shouting from a fair way off.

"Oi!" It said. "What the hell are you doing?" Oh, no, it was Slatey Brown, the colonel's gamekeeper, we were in for it now. He was marching along a row of trees towards us, in big green wellies and with smoke still coming from the end of his gun.

"Bloody hell," said Dad, "you coulda bloomin' killed us!"

"Aye," said Slatey, when he got to us, "Aye, I could anorl. Ha! Thought you were a fat squirrel. It's yer hat. Or these glasses Never seen one like that." It didn't surprise me cos Slatey had the thickest glasses I've ever seen anybody wear so I bet he hasn't seen a lot o'things. He's a bit fat anorl, is Slatey, and he was puffing and red-faced when he got to us, with a big dew drop hanging on the end of his nose. Dad was still in shock and was cuddling our Jimmy to death.

"So what you up to, then?" says Slatey.

"Well, Tom," says Dad, cos that's Slatey's real name, but no one ever calls him by it, unless they've been caught nicking one of his trees. "Well, we were looking for a Christmas tree, cos, well, money's been a bit hard come-by lately and we can't afford to buy one." Slatey took his hat off and scratched his head, and the dew-drop on the end of his nose shook and I thought it would drop... but it didn't.

"Yer still working aren't ya, Ron?"

"Aye, oh aye," said Dad, "I'm still at t'factory, but I lost me wage packet last night. Christmas wages anorl."

"Well, that's a bugger," said Slatey. I always wonder why grown ups usually believe each other and never have to say things like honest, I did, ah bet ya, honest, you ask me Dad... Not that Slatey would have asked me Grandad I don't suppose.

He looked down at me and Jimmy. "Wanted a tree did yer lads?" We didn't say ought. "Wanted one enough to steal it and risk going to prison?"

"Ey up, Tom," said me Dad, but then I caught Slatey give him a wink and then I noticed it was snowing. Great big flakes, landing on all of our heads and making us look like, oh, I dunno, funny folks with big white heads. Or a big fat white squirrel if you were Dad's head.

"Come on then, you lot," said Slatey, "I'm foggin' up 'ere, let's get back," and the dew drop fell off his nose. "And you might as well bring that damn tree. Evidence."

He took us back alongside the fence, but on his side, back to where he'd parked his Land Rover. He opened the door for Dad to get in the front then took me and Jimmy round the back.

"You lads jump in there with Dana," he said, "you'll be alright, she's usually friendly. Sit on that bale o'straw." So we climbed in and sat on the bale, which was a bit wet, next to his dog, who I suppose was called Dana. She was black, a Lab I think, and as soon as Slatey had shut the back door she came across and started licking our Jimmy's face. At least it made him laugh and stopped him moaning about his bloomin' wellies for a bit.

We had a bouncy ride back to the colonel's farm with the tree tied on the roof and I was wondering if Dad was going to be in real trouble, and get sent to prison, but I heard him and Slatey laughing in the front so I thought it would be alright. They were passing a little silver bottle back and forth to each other and drinking from it. By the time we pulled into the farmyard I was freezing, but Dad and Slatey were laughing like a pair of twits.

"Over here," said Slatey, getting out of the cab, "Just have a look at this lot," and we all jumped out and trooped into a building next to the dairy.

"Don't worry about Colonel," he said, "the old sod's away up in Scotland for Christmas, and he won't be back 'til t'New Year." Dad laughed again, and he still had Slatey's silver bottle stuck to his mouth.

Inside the building there was a great long line of turkeys. All dead and plucked and white, and hanging upside down from a rail. At the far end was a lot of boxes with taties and other stuff in. "It's all for the estate staff and some friends of the family," said Slatey. "Right then," he said, nodding towards the turkeys, "pick yourselves a good 'un, but look sharp, I've got be in Malton by one o'clock."

Me and Jimmy went down one side and Dad went down the other and we all pointed to the same turkey, right at the end, a big fat one with a few white feathers still left on its bum.

"Right you are," said Slatey, and cut it down with his pocketknife. He gave it to me and Jimmy to carry, and I got the fat end, nearly dropped it, but when I looked round for Dad to give me a hand I saw him holding a sack open while Slatey put all kinds of stuff in it from the boxes... a swede, some taties, a big cabbage, some parsnips, a bunch of carrots each about as long as my arm, and a bucketful of brussels sprouts.

"There now, that'll do yer," said Slatey, "Be a champion Christmas dinner, and we know nowt, right?"

"Right you are," said Dad. Then we all went back into t'stackyard to the Land Rover. Me and Jimmy got in the back again, and Jimmy got another good licking, then with Slatey and me Dad sat in the front we set off back to our village, making fresh tracks in the snow down all the lanes. I think the silver bottle was empty cos Slatey put it in the glove box.

"Ey, and don't say ought to Mam," said Dad, as we finished loading all the stuff into the pantry at home. "It'll be a nice surprise," and it was anorl. When Mam got back from Malton, looking tired, fed up and completely wet through with snow, and she saw our lovely big tree in the front room window, twinkling and decorated... she went all quiet. Then she took her two little bags of stuff into the pantry and had to come out again cos there was room left in there to put it. She looked at Dad, then at me and Jimmy, and said "Please tell me you've not been stealing!"

"No, love, o'course we haven't," Dad said, "it's all been given to us, free." He's right, Mam, I said.

Mam sat down on a kitchen chair and started to cry.

"Lads," said me Dad, and he gave us a look and a twitch of his head, which means go outside to lark and stay there 'til I tell you to come back in. So we did.

It wasn't quite dark yet, and our slide was covered with snow, but it made it even better, more slippery. I made Jimmy go down first, just to make sure there was no gravelly bits, and he got right to the end and hit the gate, bouncing back down the path a bit. Out the way! I shouted, and made me run up, sliding real smooth all the way down, but Jimmy hadn't got up. Ey up! I said, *Out the bloomin' way*! but it was too late, and I crashed right into him and went flying, right into the bloomin' bush.

Ow! I said. "Huh! Bloomin' ow!" he said. Right then, *Big fat bloody ow!* I said, to show him who was hurt most. Then I noticed something against me face. It was cloth. Like a cap. So much like a cap that it was one. It was Dad's. I got hold of it and turned it round. There was summat inside, some paper. An envelope. I got up and wiped off all the snow and looked at it. A brown envelope, just like a wage packet.

Hey! I said, look at this, but Jimmy was still stringin' a lot of swear words together in front of his next *Ow*. No, shurrup, look I think I've found Dad's money! And we opened the packet and took out all the notes, a lot of pounds and a few fivers, and some coins.

"It must be a *fortune*!" said Jimmy, "There must be millions!" Actually, I think you'll find there's nearly forty pounds I said, and there was. We just stared at each other. We thought for a minute about saying nowt. Maybe giving Dad the cap but keeping the money and going to Woody's shop at the corner, which was still open. We wondered how many Fruit Gums we could get for nearly forty pounds. Jimmy said he'd spend his half of the forty on comics, but then we thought we should maybe share it with Mam and Dad, half for us and half for them.

We stood there for a minute, maybe more, thinking. Well, I was thinking, but Jimmy was just starin' at the packet and grinnin' like an idiot. He's good at that.

Then I remembered it was Christmas and I said we should be honest and do the right thing. Give 'em the whole lot. Every pound. And all the coins.

Jimmy said "You what? No, hang on, Der, how about the cap and twenty pounds, and a fiver just for Mam." No, you daft sod, I said, it's all theirs. And you never know, there might be a nice reward, if we ask. So we looked at each other for another minute, then set off back up the path to the house. He had the cap, I had the wage packet. It was still snowing.

"Fifty seven thousand nine hundred and twelve," said Jimmy as we reached the back door. What you on about? I said.

"Fruit gums you could get, for forty quid." Oh, yeah, I said. Maybe you could have. Maybe.

3

The Nativity Play

I don't like school much, except, maybe, when it's getting close to Christmas, cos we don't do proper lessons then. And one year we had a new teacher.

Our proper teacher, Miss Gower, was very old, and she'd been in hospital having some very close veins taken out or summat, and it had gone a bit wrong so she was still off school, and we had a spare teacher come to us from York. Miss McDougal, and she was a bit funny. I don't think she was all there, two cups short of a tea set as Granny would say. Eric Smith said she was from Scotland so maybe they're all like that up there. And she was a bit dramatic.

The first morning she made us push all the desks back and then she pulled the old record player out of the teacher's cupboard. Miss Gower never did that cos she didn't know how to work it. She put on a record, a bit scratchy, had us doing Musical Movement, which meant she played the music and we ran about.

"Let the music flow through your body, boys and girls, and the movement will come naturally." First record was the Lone Ranger music so me and Brian Duggleby went galloping round, slapping our legs, giddy-up there! But Miss McDougal stopped us and said "Boys, boys, that is no way to treat Rossini." And she was wrong there cos his horse was called Silver.

Anyway, after that she started talking about Christmas and said we were going to do summat very special. She went round asking us what the true meaning of Christmas is, and cos she'd only been here a week she didn't know all our names. She'd point at you and say, "Tell me Richard," it's Robert, miss, "Tell me Robert, what's the true meaning of Christmas," and Robert Jackson, who's another two cups short of a tea-set says "Lights, miss." Which I thought was funny cos lights or anything bright is the last thing you think about with Robert Jackson.

I was sat with me mate, Bodger Thomas. Miss Gower had separated me and Bodge back when school started cos we were always talking and messin' about, but this new teacher didn't know that so we'd got back together. "Home for Christmas," said Bodge. The thing about Bodger is that he gets very nervous when a teacher asks him anything. He's not thick and he usually knows the right answer, but when they ask him to say it on his own in front of the whole class he seizes up. He starts to stutter and he goes all red and sweaty, and he gets in a real mess with himself.

His mam said he gets anxious, whatever the heck that is. Takes him all day to calm down sometimes, so Miss Gower never asked him stuff on his own.

Miss McDougal asked Sara Blenkinsop about Christmas next, and she said "Presents." Wrong. And then she tutted and set off towards the back of the class, towards me and Bodger.

"Oh no, I bet she asks me next!" Bodge says, digging me in the ribs. Shurrup! I said, you'll be alright. He was starting to panic.

"Oh no, bloody hell no, she's coming straight for us! Argh! Quick, stick yer hand up!" he said, "Head her off at the pass!" Shurrup, she won't ask ya. Look, she's walking t'other way now.

"So tell us all, what is the true meaning of Christmas, er, you!" and she swung round and pointed straight at Bodge.

"Aw Jesus," he said.

"Yes, that's *right*!" says Miss McDougal, "Jesus. The true meaning of Christmas, children, is Jesus. And so what we're going to do today and for the rest of this week is prepare a nativity play!"

"A what?" says Bodge. It's Mary and Joseph and them lot, I said, in the stable with baby Jesus and that manger thing, you know, like they have outside church. On the grassy bit outside the church every year there's a manger and straw and these dummies standing about, like religious scarecrows. They have paper mashy faces and this year Joseph was kneeling down, but somebody had kicked his head in. It might have been Bodger come to think of it.

So anyway, Miss McDougal pulled out a big trunk full of costumes and opened up the drama cupboard where we keep all the pretend swords and stuff, and she starts to pick the team. It's a musical she said, so the good singers would obviously get the best parts.

Bodger can't sing for toffee so he got himself a cushy number back stage as her special helper. Most of the girls were stable animals, such as cows and sheep and a few hens. Then she picked three lads for wise men and three more for shepherds, but then Jennifer Baker, who can be a right gobby little sod, started giving her some grief. She said "Never mind Scotland but round here women can be shepherds anorl," cos her mother was one. So Jennifer became a fourth shepherd and grabbed herself a big crook from the cupboard.

Skinny little Wendy Somerset, or Wetton Windy as we called her, a right teacher's pet, got to play Mary, and that was a daft choice cos Mary never wore glasses. Course, she was capped, little miss cleverclogs, smiling fit to make you sick she was. Nobody likes her.

"And now then, finally, for our Joseph we'll have..." and her finger went sweeping round the class, and all the lads who hadn't yet been picked looked at the floor, so I did anorl.

"You!" she said, and when I looked up her finger was pointing right between me eyes.

"Oh God," I said.

"No, Joseph!" says Bodger, laughing and giving me a shove, so when she'd turned round I flicked his boil with me ruler.

For the next three days we practised the play over and over and it was a real strain. She told us what to say and where to stand but it kept getting too crowded round the manger and I was fed up with people standing on me toes.

And in the films, like when Elvis is going to sing, it just sort of happens, real natural. One minute they're talking and the next minute he's singing and it's good. But in our play it was crap. Like, for instance, I had to say Oh Mary, where ever shall we stay tonight with weather so cold and horrid in this bleak mid-Winter, and then there'd be a pause while Mrs Dicker would get going on the piano and eventually we'd all sing *In the Bleak Mid-Winter*.

And Brian Duggleby was a shepherd and he said See, by yonder hedgerow, how pretty the holly and the ivy doth grow. Then we'd launch into *The Holly and the Ivy*. But anybody who's ever kept sheep knows the last thing you want 'em near is bloomin' ivy cos it's bad for 'em.

Miss McDougal couldn't think how to introduce *Good King Wenceslas* cos he wasn't even in the story, but we sang it anyway. Wetton Wendy got to sing the big hit of the show, *Silent Night*, and what she said before it started was Oh Joseph, how peaceful our dear sweet baby Jesus looks in the manger, all is calm and bright, what a beautifully silent night.

Silent? She'd obviously never been in a foldyard when you've got sheep, cows, hens and pigs all in t'same corner. And it didn't make sense, cos she had to sing *round yon virgin*. Yon virgin? Well, she was supposed to be the bloomin' virgin, and there wasn't another one as far as I know. Me Dad said he'd bet there wasn't one at all in our village. And when she sang the bit about Holy infant so tender and mild we would all sing Holy insect, which put her off and she'd get real mad.

Mrs Dicker played the piano like Ringo plays the drums. She banged away so hard it would move, so after every song she'd get Bodger to help her push it back up against the wall. She was the vicar's wife so you had to watch your language round her. Her husband was Mr Dicker the vicar, or Vicar Dicker as he was known round here. And he was a bit thick. Me Dad said he was so thick that being a vicar was the only job he could get, and he used to say to me and our Jimmy, when we did ought daft, you're as thick as Vicar Dicker.

Any road, after we'd practised everything to death, the big day came. The play would start at seven o'clock at night, and all the mams and dads were going to watch.

On the afternoon we went down to the village hall for what Miss McDougal said was a dress rehearsal, but nobody wore dresses, not even the girls. Everybody had dressing gowns on, all different colours, some were tartan, and tea towels round their heads, like they did back in Jesus' time.

Mr Schofield the school janitor rigged up some lights. Well, when I say some lights I mean every bloomin' light he could get his hands on. There were desk lights and reading lights, inspection lights and table lamps, all fastened to the ceiling above the stage with string and wire and sticky tape. He even had a few car headlamps at the front, pointing straight in our eyes, run from a big battery. When he turned it all on it was so bright you couldn't see a thing, and the kettle stopped working in the kitchen, which didn't please the Mothers Union who were in there doing all the sandwiches and stuff.

It was as bright as the middle of a bonfire, all of us on the stage were squinting and bashing into each other, like piglets under a pig lamp.

"That's good," said Miss McDougal, "as you won't be able to see the audience so you won't get nervous or be distracted."

"No, maybe not," said Eric Smith, "but we'll get third degree burns!"

One of Bodger's jobs, well, his only job, was to open and close the curtains, which he did by pulling on a rope at the side, in what they call the wings. The curtains were closed at first and we'd all pile on stage and fight and shove each other out of the way so we'd get best place, Mr Schofield turned his lights on, then he'd open the curtains and off we'd go.

After a couple of goes Miss McDougal seemed to get a bit tired, and said it would just have to do. She wasn't happy with the baby Jesus, and that's probably cos we hadn't got one. It was just a rolled up white blanket. After Wetton Windy sang *Silent Night* she picked up Jesus out of the manger, cuddled him a bit and said a few words then the curtains closed - The End.

But the long skinny bundle kept flopping over and it looked daft. Miss McDougal told Bodger to find something to wrap in the blanket before we started at night, "Something to give it more life and feel, a bit of weight." He went off to get summat and we packed in for the day. As we were walking home for our teas I asked Bodge what he'd wrapped up as baby Jesus.

"A concrete block," he said.

At home our Jimmy kept calling me Joseph all through tea so when me Mam wasn't looking I gave him a slap and he started crying. She threatened to send me upstairs to stay there all night, even if it meant missing the play.

"Oh aye," said Dad, "and where does that leave Mary, an umarried mother?"

"She wouldn't be t'first round here," said Mam. Anyway, I had to say sorry to Jimmy and promise to save them all a good seat on the front row.

I ran back to the village hall for half past six, like Miss McDougal said, and everyone was in the side room getting their costumes on. She was putting makeup on all the girls, black stuff on their eyelashes and red lipstick, bright orange cheeks and yellow powder. Wetton Windy looked like a goldfish.

"And for my little men," said Miss McDougal, "we'll have beards and mustaches." Wor, that's great, we all thought, but then she just stuck her hand up the fireplace chimney and wiped soot on our faces. Brian Duggleby started licking his and said it tasted a bit like burnt bacon. I just felt mucky. Then it was time to make a start so we all had to be quiet. Sort of.

"Are there many in the audience?" whispered Miss McDougal.

"Aye, it's swarm wick," said Bodge. The hall was full to bursting and they brought in extra chairs. Me Mam and Dad and our Jimmy were right up front and they'd given him a big bag o'Maltesers the lucky sod. Mrs Dicker was thumping away at a few hymns and Mr Schofield had tied the piano to the wall with some rope to stop it moving.

We had to go through the kitchen to get to the back of the stage, and there were stacks o'potted meat sandwiches and biscuits and jugs of orange juice and great big tea pots all ready for afterwards. Bodge grabbed a handful of custard creams as he went past.

We all got on stage, with the curtain closed, and Mrs Dicker banged out the starting music, *Once in Royal David's City*, and Mr Schofield started plugging in and flicking all his switches and it got real hot and bright. I could feel meself starting to sweat already, and this bloomin' tea towel on me head was only making it worse. Wetton Windy had left her glasses off cos she thought it made her look prettier, and she was trying to blink but her eye makeup was getting sticky and every other blink didn't work. Her eyelashes were stickin' together. It looked like she was trying to wake up.

Miss McDougal wished us all good luck then went back into the wing and told Bodger to open the curtains. I could see him start pulling on the rope, but nowt happened.

"Curtain!" said Miss McDougal.

"I am!" says Bodge. And he was pulling away and not getting anywhere. We were all starting to sweat on stage now, it was like an incubator and worse with the curtains being kept shut.

"Open those curtains, boy! *Now!*" she shouts and Bodge had got a bit upset and panicky, "Am am am I b-b-bloody am!" he said and gave the rope a real big pull. There was a loud shriek from somewhere up in the top of the curtains and a rat's tail fell onto the stage. The shrieking kept going as Bodger pulled the curtains open, then it was just a squeal, then it stopped. "Bloody rat stuck in it," said Bodge, but miss McDougal was chewing on her hankie and seemed to be thinking about summat else.

We started the play and got to the first song all right. The mams and dads were all enjoying it and clapping loudly after every bit, but we couldn't see anything for the lights. It was getting hotter, and these woolly dressing gowns were real itchy. Brian Duggleby looked like he'd run ten miles, all red-faced and sweaty. He sat down on a paper mashy bolder, and it crumpled under his weight, but we carried on.

I sang my part of *In the Bleak Mid Winter* and forgot some words but the piano was so loud I don't think anybody noticed. All the girls' makeup was starting to run, and some of them really did look like cows now. Or panda bears.

28

Wetton Windy had her eyes closed most of the time, cos I don't think she could get 'em open anymore, and it made her look like she was in a trance. Mind, I've seen pictures of Mary looking like that.

The sweat was rolling down me face and stinging me eyes now, and all the shepherds were lying down, among the sheep, and the three kings were leaning against the back wall. Crowns had all fallen off. We finally got to the last song, *Silent Night*, and just before she started singing, I heard one of the shepherds say to Wetton Windy, "Holy insect! Holy insect! *Holy insect!*"

She started singing, eyes glued shut, and she stepped forward, banging into the manger. "*Silent night, holy night*," and even Mrs Dicker had toned down the piano to make it sound nice.

I could see Miss McDougal off at the side, smiling and swaying to the music, her hands waving in the air as if she was conducting. "*All is calm, all is bright...*" Windy was making a meal of it, the clever little sod. Her mam and dad were sat next to mine and I bet they were smirkin'. She was swaying as well now, "*Round yon virgin mother and child...*" and then she said it. She actually said it, no, she *sang* it.

"*Holy insect so tender and mild.*" The shepherds started sniggering and poking each other, the wise men turned their faces to the back wall and laughed. Even the cows and sheep looked up and started to giggle. I was trembling and biting me lip. And she just carried on singing the rest of the song, eyes tight shut, as if nothing had happened. Miss McDougal looked puzzled and I think she was asking Bodger if he'd heard anything unusual.

At the end she still got a big clap from the audience and when it stopped she came right up close to me and bent over into the manger to get the baby Jesus. I looked across at Bodge and I think I saw him wink at me.

She slipped her hands under the bundle and was slowly lifting the baby Jesus out. Or at least she was trying to.

Everything was dead quiet, waiting for the big finish. She bent down further into the manger, and got both her arms right under the blanket and lifted. It slowly rose an inch... then fell down again. She changed her grip, grabbing two big handfuls of blanket on either side and gave a grunt, and with her cheeks blown right out and her red lips puckered up like a chicken's bum, she tried again. Slowly... very slowly... she straightened up, and heaved the bundle out of the manger and up to her chest.

She was supposed to say "Little baby Jesus, lord of all..." and that was it. But she didn't. She started to stagger instead. She was losing her grip on the blanket and suddenly let go. And the concrete block fell out of the blanket and right onto my foot.

Now, different people say different things when they get hurt. You don't have to think it up it just comes straight out. Some people just say Ouch, or Ooh. Our Jimmy says Ooya-ooya, just like that. And Dad, when he traps his finger or summat, sounds like an old sheep, and says Baaaastard! Me, I usually say Ow bugger! Usually.

But I'd been spending a lot of time with Bodger lately and he says something different and I supposed I must have picked it up, cos when the concrete block hit me foot I said *Ow f***!*

Yes, the very naughty f-word. Loud and clear.

Well, if you thought it was quiet when Mary was about to pick baby Jesus up, it was even quieter now. Until I started hopping. Me foot was killing me. I thought I'd broke all the bones. Maybe I should have said something, to finish the play and get us off, something like Behold the baby Jesus, a solid little king.

I really did think about saying that but I got mad when I caught sight of Wetton Windy grinning away at me with her eyes shut, like she was really enjoying it, so I just said *You stupid cow!*

I'd forgotten about the play and I didn't notice me tea-towel come off, but I heard Miss McDougal shouting at Bodger to close the curtains, *quickly*! And he couldn't. The dead rat had jammed up the works and the curtains wouldn't budge.

Mr Schofield tried to get onto the stage to turn off all his lights, and some of 'em had started to smoke, but there were shepherds and wise men lying all over the place and he kept stepping on them. He tripped over Brian Duggleby, went full length and banged his head on the manger. More bad words.

There wasn't much silent night left now, everybody was howling with laughter, except Miss McDougal. Even Vicar Dicker was laughing and the audience was so loud you could hardly hear Mrs Dicker who was also sweatin' now and pounding *Jingle Bells* to death.

We didn't stay for the sandwiches and biscuits. Me Mam said we had to get home, smartish, limping or not, and she said if our Jimmy didn't stop laughing he'd get the same good hiding I was going to get. On the way out we passed

Miss McDougal sat in a little heap on the front steps, wafting a damp lace hankie in front of her face. It was starting to rain.

"Merry Christmas!" me Dad said as we went past. But she didn't say anything. Well, maybe they don't in Scotland.

4

Present Company

It wasn't my fault, but we'd been sent outside to lark 'til tea time. Me Mam said she had a lot to do and we were getting on her nerves. But me Dad wasn't sent outside and I know he was getting on her nerves just as bad, and he's twice as much as we are put together.

Anyway, it was Christmas Eve and we'd already watched *Mr McGoo's Christmas Carol*, and had some treacle samwidges, so I didn't much mind. Best thing was... it was snowing!

The slide we'd made on our front path wasn't up to much now, specially since Dad had thrown a shovelful of ashes down it. So we walked up the street to the village green to lark on the kissing gate. This was at the top of Abbey Lane, a road that nobody used, and it went round the back of the church, up past the old cemetery and it was a bit scary. A lot scary when it got dark. The older kids said that a zombie lived in the old cemetery and sometimes came out at night to swing on the gate, making it creak and squeal like a cat being skinned alive.

It was snowing like mad now, and starting to get dark, and Jimmy kept daring me to go up the lane a bit further. So what we did was make a slide, starting at the bottom of the lane and adding a bit to the top after every go. Slowly working our way up, bit by bit, into the dark, out of the streetlights. Never getting very far away from each other. Snow was so thick that our feet were like snow ploughs, shoving piles of it in front of us when we came down.

Finally, we'd got all the way up to the kissing gate and tried to have a swing, but the snow was real deep there and it wouldn't even open. Right, I said, one last big slide then we'll go home. I went first, running like mad, and set off down the lane. It was real slape by now and I was down at the bottom in half a second.

Then Jimmy came, and for once he could slide faster and further than me. See, I had wellies on, which are rubbish for slidin' but, because he'd kicked up a fuss about losing his big socks down his wellies, me Mam had let him wear his old shoes, and they had no grips left on 'em, so he shot down that slide like stink.

"Ey up Der!" he shouted as he whipped past me. He went right off the end of the slide onto the gravelly stuff and stopped real sharp. Well, his feet stopped, but his top half kept going and he took off, flying through the air, through all the snowflakes, and then he landed, *Whumph!* in a big snow drift.

Ha! Ya great daft beggar! I said, and I thought I'd have to get all the snow out of his neck before he started crying, but he never said a word. He didn't move...

He just laid there. Jim? I said. Come on, gerrup. But he just laid there, with snow coming down, covering his black jacket and making it go all white. Jimmy! *Gerrup will ya!*

I walked across and when I got there I could see it wasn't a real snowdrift, it was an old tree stump just covered with a bit o'snow. He'd smashed right into it.

About every single day of my life, since I was three, I'd heard me Mam say I wasn't to do daft stuff, like run over cobbles, or climb big trees or jump over fences... cos I'd split me head open. And I suddenly knew that's what Jimmy had done. He'd gone and split his bloomin' head open on that tree stump! I'd never seen a real head split open, and I really didn't fancy it, specially now, and specially here, with nobody about, and with it snowing like mad, in the dark... and tea time.

I reached down and thumped his shoulder. Jimmy? Come on, stop mucking about, we have to go, it's blizzardin' and we'll be late for tea! He didn't move. I knelt down and rolled him over, shutting me eyes cos if his head was split open I didn't want to see what was inside. Jim? Y'alright? *Jimmy!* He still never said anything, so I opened me eyes and looked. He was a bit pale. Well, white really, but no blood. Not even a bruise. I couldn't see any hole in his head, or even a mark, but I thought he was dead, and just as I was about to run away I saw a bit o'fog come out of his mouth. It was *breath!* He was alive!

Jim, can you gerrup? I said. He didn't even try. I knew I had to shift him or he'd be buried in snow, and I knew I wasn't supposed to leave him. There was nobody about, no cars coming past or anything, nothing... just a big shadow coming down Abbey Lane. Eh? Yeah, a great big shadow, coming slowly towards me! *Argh! It was the zombie!*

Oh I just knew it! He was going to eat Jimmy, cos that's what they do! Before I could get back up on me feet it was right there, big and black, leaning over me!

"What's up, young fella?" it said. Well, it wasn't a real zombie. It was a tramp. An old one with a long beard and a big black coat with a hood on. It's, er, it's me brother, Jimmy, he's banged his head and won't gerrup, I said. We were sliding.

"Oh, aye?" said the tramp, "Let's have a look," and he bent down next to Jimmy. He opened Jim's eyelid and then put a finger on his neck, like I've seen Dr Kildare do on the telly. "Well, he's still with us," he said, "but it's been a nasty fall. Where do you boys live?"

Down there, I said, pointing across t'green and down the village. Number 53. Me Mam and Dad are there. And with that the old tramp had Jimmy scooped up and sort of covered in a blanket he'd pulled from off his shoulders.

He set off through the snow with me trying to keep up. I was hoping he didn't think it was all my fault, cos it weren't. Jimmy's younger than me, I said, I'm supposed to look after him. Do you think me Mam'll kill me? The tramp laughed. He seemed nice enough, much better than any zombie would have been, I thought. If he dies will I go to prison? Will me Mam kill me? I said.

"Oh no, lad," he said, "not tonight, not on Christmas Eve." Oh, right, I thought, 'appen she'll wait while Boxing Day.

We walked up our front path, and the snow was real deep by now, so I had to follow the tramp's footprints just to get through. When Dad opened the back door to us he just gawped, and said "What the...?" It's Jimmy, I said, he went off the slide and smashed into a tree stump and this man's helped me carry him back.

"Oh good lord, come in come in!" said Dad, stepping back to make way into the kitchen, but Mam suddenly appeared and got in the way. For a second she looked as white as Jimmy.

"Whatever have you done?" she cried, but Dad pulled her back.

"Away love, let 'em get inside so we can see." We all went in. Dad took the blanket off Jimmy, and in the kitchen light I could see it was red now, but that meant seeing any blood on it would be hard work.

"I think it's just mild concussion," said the tramp, "he's breathing regular and he's got a good pulse, no sign o'blood, nowt broken that I can see, just badly winded I reckon. Best get him out o'these wet clothes and warmed up by t'fire."

He was right. By the time Mam had Jimmy undressed and into a blanket by the fire with a mug of cocoa, he was all woken up and right as rain.

The old tramp had been sitting quietly on a chair by the kitchen door, and apart from the cup o'tea Mam gave him we'd all but forgotten about him. Then Mam said he should have some food with us. He said no thanks, at first, then Dad told him it was getting worse out there, a real snowstorm, and that he'd need some hot grub inside him to keep warm, so in the end he said thank-you and yes. But first he said he should have a wash, so Mam got him a big towel and some fancy new soap that smelled like raspberries.She ran him a sinkful of hot water and we all went into the front room to leave him to it.

Ten minutes later, me and Jimmy crept back into the kitchen to watch him. He was having a bowl of stew and dumplings Mam had made for our teas, and he was spooning it into a hole in his great big beard, which looked white now he'd had a wash.

We sat down at the kitchen table with him and while we had our teas he started telling us stories, about where he'd been and the jobs he'd had. He knew where robins sleep at night and how far a fox can run in a day, and why the moon gets bigger and smaller, where the river starts from... He knew loads o'stuff. I asked where he was going next, and he looked down at his feet, at his big toes sticking through a pair of matching holes in his green socks, and he smiled.

"We'll just have to see," he said.

Jimmy asked him where he came from.

"Oh, here and there," he said. And when Jimmy asked how old he was, he just said "As old as me tongue and a bit older than me teeth" and laughed.

After tea I went through to the front room, to see if the Christmas film had started and I heard Mam and Dad talking quietly about the old man having nowhere to go, and this being Christmas eve and all. And snowing like mad.

"It's no night to be travelling or dossing down in a barn," said Dad.

"No, and he's not going to," said Mam, "He can sleep here, on the settee. We've plenty of bedding."

Just as the film was starting, all the electric went out and it was pitch black.

"Ey up," said Dad, "snow's finally brought them lines down. Let me find some matches," but before he'd even got out of the chair a flash of light lit the room and suddenly the old tramp had a candle lit. He put it into the brass candlestick on the mantle piece, and we all just looked.

"That's 'andy," said Dad, "Well done!"

Mam got a few more candles out and Dad banked the fire up to keep us cosy. We had no telly so they talked. Well, the old man talked. He told us more stories, and they were always funny and had happy endings. He talked about all the Christmas Eves he'd had and the people he'd spent 'em with. But he never mentioned the presents he got. Maybe he never got any.

Mam said they should have a drink for Christmas, so Dad and the old man had a tot of Lamb's Navy rum apiece and she poured herself a glass of Bristol Cream sherry, then topped up me and Jimmy's mugs from the cocoa jug on the hearth.

The tramp stood up and raised his glass. "I'll make a toast, if I might," he said. Mam and Dad just looked at each other, but let him get on with it. "To friends in need and friends in deed, and to the wonderous Christmas spirit that lives within these walls!" It was a lot posher than anything else he'd said all night, but Mam and Dad stood up and clinked their glasses with his.

"Merry Christmas!" he said, and then patting me and Jim on the head and clinking our cocoa mugs, he leaned down and said it again, *Merry Christmas!*

Next thing I knew the clock was striking eleven and Mam said it was well past bedtime. We said we had to leave some supper for Father Christmas, when he came down the chimney, a mince pie and a glass of sherry, like always, but the old man said we had to look outside first to see what the weather was doing.

He said that depending on the weather, Father Christmas liked different things. If it was raining he liked one thing, and if it was foggy he'd like another. We all looked out the window and it was still snowing.

"Ee, it's heavens high," Mam said.

"Hoss-belly deep," said Dad.

"So, tonight is very special, it should be his favourite," said the old man, "Tonight he'll be wanting a glass of brandy, a sausage roll, and three chocolate biscuits." Dad laughed and Mam said she thought we could manage that, and we went into the kitchen. A minute later she was back with it all ready on a tray and lay it in the hearth. But I think it was rum instead of brandy. I'm sure wouldn't mind.

We really liked listening to the stories, and didn't want to go to bed, but Mam made us finish our cocoa and we finally said goodnight to the old man. Mam took us upstairs with a candle and made us promise not to get up too early. Seven o'clock at the earliest, and to be quiet when we did.

Then she went back downstairs and we heard her and Dad saying goodnight to the old man, and asking if he'd be alright on the settee. Then they both came up to bed, and I could hear 'em whispering, but soon the house was all quiet. We kept the candle on in our room.

I had a real funny dream that night, but as soon as I woke up it was gone and I couldn't remember a thing, except that it felt good. The candle had burned out. Jimmy was still asleep but it was already light outside.

I looked out the window and the snow was really deep now. It had buried the dustbin and you couldn't even see where the path was. It was all quiet. Not a sound.

"Merry Christmas, sleepy heads!" It was Mam at the bedroom door. "You two have had a good sleep, it's gone nine, the latest you've ever slept on Christmas morning! Are you alright Jim?" he was, just a bit dozy, as usual. "We've got the electric back on," she said, "so I'll go down and make some tea and toast, and we'll see if Father Christmas has been, eh?"

We got our dressing gowns on and met Dad on the landing, then all four of us went downstairs, with Mam shushing us in case the old man was still asleep. But when we opened the front room door he wasn't there. The bedding was all neatly folded up on the settee, but there was no sign of him.

"He's not in t'kitchen neither," said Dad, "or the pantry, but he can't have got far, not in all this snow." Mam had gone all quiet. She was staring at the mantlepiece.

"Ron?" she said, and she never called him Ron. She whispered to him, but I could hear. "Did you fill these stockings with presents?"

"No, love" he said, "and I didn't hang 'em there. I've never even seen 'em before."

"Me neither," she said. They just stood there, staring. Dad was scratching his head.

"He's been then!" said Jimmy, "He's been and left us presents and did he have his supper?" We looked down, and the tray was empty, just a few crumbs left on the plate. And a small note, written in red crayon. It said *Thank-you, kindly. Merry Christmas!*

Dad had gone through to the kitchen and was shouting back at us, "Ey, come and see this!" We all went through and he had the back door wide open. The snow was about three feet deep and starting to fall inside.

"Look there," he said. Where, Dad? I said, I can't see owt but snow.

"Aye, that's just what I mean!" Dad said. "No footprints, not a mark. He can't have left through here. And t'bathroom's empty."

"Maybe he used the front door," said Mam, and I suppose he didn't know that we weren't supposed to use the front door unless we had posh company. Stupid rule.

"No love, I've been to t'front door and it's just same, nobody's been through there, not a single footprint, nowt but deep snow. It's a mystery how he's gone. Vanished!"

Jimmy whispered to me that we should go and look under our bed. Don't be stupid! I said, didn't you see the bloomin' size of him?

Mam and Dad were still wandering about, looking behind curtains and doors and in among all the coats on the rack. Dad even opened the cupboard under the stairs and stuck his head in there for a look. Mam told him not to be so daft, but she didn't seem to have any better ideas.

I said What about up in the attic, Dad, have you looked up there? I knew he hadn't cos to get into the attic you have to go out to the coalhouse and fetch the stepladder, and he hadn't done that. And he wouldn't want to.

"People don't just vanish," said Mam, "He has to be somewhere. Where have you looked?"

"Everywhere!" said Dad, "I've look every bloomin' where and he's disappeared!"

We all just stood still for a minute. I thought there might be an argument about it all, cos me Mam and Dad don't like mysteries. They have to know about stuff. When me and Jimmy did something we shouldn't have done, and we didn't admit to it, they'd would always say "I'll get to the bottom of this!" And sometimes they did. But it wasn't like that right now. This missing tramp was different. A bit scary. Nobody said anything.

"I know!" said Jimmy, and he called us all back into the front room. He pointed at the fireplace. "I bet he went up the chimney and got a lift with Father Christmas!"

"Aye lad," said Dad, "'appen he did just that!" Then everyone went real quiet.

5

What the Dickens?

"Ooh look," said Mam, kicking me Dad on the leg, but not very hard.

"What is it now?" he said, still reading the paper.

"*A Christmas Carol*'s on telly tomorrow night, the real one with Alastair Sim."

"Well block my 'airy nose with a radish," said Dad, winking at me, "who'd a'thought they'd put that on at this time o'year?"

"No need to be sarcastic. We're watching it, alright?" she said in her "and that's final" voice, which worked just as well on Dad as it did on me and our Jimmy.

We'd just been doing Charles Dickens at school. Charles Dickens wrote that film, I said.

"That's right, lad, he did," said me Dad, "and d'you know what else?"

What? I said.

"Ebenezer Scrooge came from Malton."

"Rubbish!" said Mam.

Did he really, Dad, that stingy old Scrooge, did he come from Malton?

"Aye, lad, he was yer mother's grandad. He-heh!" Me Dad was asking for a clout, and I waited for Mam to say summat, but she still had her head stuck in the *Radio Times*.

She tutted. "Your father's more full o'rubbish than Peasey Hill tip." Our Jimmy laughed. Peasey Hill tip was one of our best places to lark, but we weren't supposed to go there.

"Scrooge never came from Malton at all, and neither did Charles Dickens." Me Dad suddenly folded his paper with a lot of noise. He does this. Some people, when they're getting into an argument, say things like "Now hold on a minute," or "Hey, now look here..." but Dad just folds his newspaper with a lot of noise. And he folds it and folds it, and folds it, until it's just a small square, well past what it's supposed to fold up like. You could get it in your pocket.

"And before you start," she said to him, "I'll have you know I once did a school project on *A Christmas Carol*."

Then our Jimmy folded his comic up, trying to be like Dad, but he didn't make ought like as much noise, and he tore the back page. We waited for Dad to say summat, cos we knew he would.

He leaned right forward, almost out of his chair. "Ebenezer Scrooge was a bookkeeper who worked in Malton at t'back o't'picture house," he said, "and that's *right*." He should have put his tongue out, like we do at school, then she would have known he was right.

"Good grief, here we go," said Mam, closing the Radio Times, quietly, and straightening out her pinny. She looked at me and Jimmy. "I sometimes wonder if your father ever went to school." I could see where this was going.

Me Mam had gone up to the Grammar School when she was a girl, which was quite posh, and me Granny still talks about her in the lovely uniform. But me Dad had gone to some little school that wasn't posh, in Pickering, and I don't think he went there very often.

"A lot o'folks think that Scrooge came from Malton," she said.

"An' a lot o'folks is right then," said Dad.

"But," she said, "It was just the idea for Scrooge's office that came from Malton. That's all. His office ..."

I was trying to think what Scrooge's office looked like cos it had been ages since I'd seen the film, but I couldn't think.

"How the 'eck can an office come from anywhere?" said Dad. "Eh?"

"What I mean is, the office Dickens described in his novel was based on a real office that Dickens once went to in Malton." Mam was talking in her posh voice now, but I don't know where the film went and this novel thing came in. She seemed to have Dad on the ropes now so she carried on, "He had a friend worked there. And yes, I'll grant you, it was behind the cinema in Chancery Lane. Still is, in fact."

"Well it would be his friend that was Scrooge, then," said Dad.

"Is 'e dead, Mam?" said Jimmy, who was scared stiff o'Scrooge cos I'd seen him hide behind the settee last time the film was on.

"Yes, he is," said Mam, "Well, what I mean is, he was never really alive cos it was all made up. It's just a story, love."

"Just a story my bald aunt fanny," said Dad. I could see he was getting het up. He believes in Father Christmas does me Dad, so I suppose that thinking Scrooge is real comes quite easy.

"You won't have it will you?" said Mam, "So, we'll find out once and for all then, shall we? We'll go to the authority," and she went over to the bureau and got her writing pad out. "Pen!" she said, and Dad got the Biro from behind his ear and chucked it to her.

"Right you two," she said, after she'd spent two minutes writing summat, "you just take this note round to Mr Fenwick, you know where he lives don't you?"

Oh, we knew alright. He lives up Cemetery Lane, the only house up there, right next to all the graves. The scariest house in the village. Nobody ever went there. Not even Magson's dog and it goes everywhere.

"If anyone knows what's what about Charles Dickens, it's Mr Fenwick," said Mam, folding the note and sticking it out to me. "He was the best teacher that Grammar School ever had, shame to see him retire, but he's still worth three of them that's wastin' chalk up there now. Get your coats and wellies on and take that torch from the cupboard under the stairs." she was serious.

She wouldn't usually let us out at this time of night on our own. Even the shop was shut. And she was sending us up Cemetery Lane, in the dark. That's scary, maybe dangerous. I wondered if we'd be getting paid for it.

"Now then, give that note to Mr Fenwick, don't forget your please and thank-yous, and he'll tell you all about Charles Dickens. Then come back here and we'll try and drum it into that ignorant father of yours." She opened the back door, made sure Jimmy's scarf was tight, then shoved us outside. "And save them torch batteries," she said as she shut the door.

It was freezing cold, and so dark that the streetlights seemed to be struggling to stay on.

"Ey, this is alright, Der," said Jimmy, "off out by oursens." Aye, I said, but you wait 'til we get to Cemetery Lane, ya won't be so keen then. And he wasn't. When we walked past Hunter's Hall and got to the bottom of the lane, I'm sure it got even darker. There were no streetlights up there. It seemed just the right time for an owl to hoot, or a fox to scream somewhere over a field.

I shone the torch up the lane, but the light didn't go very far. Anyway, we set off, real careful. I don't know how it happened, but I suddenly noticed I was holding our Jimmy's hand.

"Are ya scared, Der?" he said. Well, what are you supposed to say to that? To a younger brother? So I said nowt. Then I said, No, I aren't scared... not much.

Funny thing was, he didn't mind holding hands, and neither did I. We kept doing it.

Mr Fenwick's was the only house on Cemetery Lane, up past some sheds and a fallen down greenhouse. They were all full of black shadows and strange, quiet noises that I didn't want our Jimmy to know about. I didn't want to know about 'em either. I kept the torch pointed down at the lane in front of us, and walked as quick as I could. I didn't even stop to pick up what looked like a penny down among some gravel.

Finally we got to the front door, and the house was all dark. I reached up and got hold of his knocker. It was hard and cold, and shaped like a lion's head, and when I knocked it was loud.

"Is it going to turn into an ugly face, like that ghost in the film?" said Jimmy. No it bloody it isn't! I said, and knocked again, even louder, just to show I wasn't scared. I let go of his hand.

From somewhere inside there was a little yapping noise that came closer and closer, then we heard somebody messing about behind the door, scratching and banging and undoing bolts and so on. Then it opened and we stepped back a bit, and we were suddenly holding hands again, though it wasn't my idea. Mr Fenwick was stood there, holding a candle and looking down at us. He was tall. And old. Very old. The yapping thing was a Jack Russell who ran out between Mr Fenwick's legs and stuck its nose up Jimmy's trouser leg, and wouldn't take it out.

Er, hello mister Fenwick, I said.

"Why, hello, hello... er, it's Derek, isn't it? And yes, yes, your brother James. Hello boys, hello boys, so nice to see you, are you carol singing?" No, I said, we came with a message from me Mam, and I shoved the note at him.

"Ah yes," he said, "ah yes, come in, come in and let's see what's to do."

We went in and closed the door behind us, and walked along his front passage, it was a bit dark. Mr Fenwick was in front, then me, then Jimmy, then the Jack Russell, and we ended up in his sitting room. It was still a bit dark, only three candles and an oil lamp going, and there was no Christmas decorations up or anything. Just thousands of books. Not just on shelves but everywhere.

"Sit down, sit down," he said, and I thought there's no need to keep saying everything twice just cos there's two of us, we can both hear at t'same time. We moved some books and sat on the settee, while he read the note.

Jimmy leaned over to me and whispered, "He's had a lot o'birthdays 'asn't he, Der?" Shurrup, I said.

"Your mother's asking about Dickens' *Christmas Carol*, I see," he said. "And how is your mother, is she well, is she well?" Yes, thank-you, I said.

"Yes, thank-you," said Jimmy.

"Would you boys like a mint?" and he passed me this old box with a lid on, the kind that usually has cigarettes in when you see 'em in a film. Thank-you, I said, and I took one out then passed it along to Jimmy. "Thank-you," he said. I popped it in me mouth and right away I knew it was one of them Extra Strong Old English Mints. Bugger! Kids aren't supposed to have them. This was going to hurt and I should have stopped our Jimmy getting one cos he'll be screaming in a minute, but too late. He'd popped it straight in and was sucking.

"Now then, boys, Charles Dickens. Your mother was a good scholar during her years at our school, and she helped me do considerable research into that most celebrated of our nineteenth century novelists."

I wasn't sure what he was on about, but I was doing better than our Jimmy who was going cross-eyed and chewing on his sleeve. This was his first ever Old English Mint. Probably his last anorl.

Mr Fenwick pulled a pipe down from a rack on the mantelpiece and stuck it in his mouth. "Well now. Charles Dickens was born on Friday, February 7, 1812, at Landport, a suburb of Portsmouth. That's way down south, you know. His father, John, was a clerk in the navy pay-office attached to the dockyard, and his mother was Elizabeth Dickens."

It all seemed a bloody long way from Scrooge and Tiny Tim, and I was bustin' to get back outside and get shot of this mint. Jimmy was smiling again, though his eyes were watering, and he was still wiping his mouth on his sleeve. He was watching the terrier, who seemed to be lickin' its chops a lot, and coughing.

Old Fenwick rattled on. "The Dickens family moved to London when Charles was two. John had a poor head for finances, and in 1824 found himself imprisoned for debt. Young Charles was put to work at Warren's Blacking Factory and had his first taste of child labour."

I was thinking that child labour would taste a lot better than this mint. I was beginning to wish I'd brought one of me Dad's hankies. And when's Scrooge going to show up? Maybe I should ask him and get done with it.

"When the family finances were put at least partly to rights and his father was released, the twelve-year-old Dickens, already scarred psychologically by the experience, was further wounded by his mother's insistence that he continue to work at the factory. His father, however, rescued him from that dreadful fate, and between 1824 and 1827 Dickens was a day pupil at a school in London." It must be nearly midnight, I was thinking, when's he gonna shurrup?

I noticed Jimmy was missing. I think he'd followed the dog through into the kitchen. I bet they both wanted some water, and old Fenwick hadn't seen 'em leave. He rattled on. "At fifteen, he found employment as an office boy at an attorney's, while he studied shorthand at night. His brief stint at the Blacking Factory haunted him all of his life but the dark secret became a source both of creative energy and of the preoccupation with the themes of alienation and betrayal, which would emerge, most notably, in David Copperfield and in Great Expectations." Excuse me, mister Fenwick, I said.

"Yes, Derek?" He did write *A Christmas Carol* didn't he?

"Indeed he did. *A Christmas Carol* was the first of Dickens' enormously successful Christmas books, each intended as, and I quote him: 'a whimsical sort of masque intended to awaken loving and forbearing thoughts.'" Aye, righto then, I said, and did Scrooge come from Malton?

"Good heavens, my boy, no he didn't. *The Pickwick Papers*, published on New Year's Eve in 1836, had contained as a good-humoured Christmas chapter *The Story of the Goblins Who Stole a Sexton*. The tale's protagonist, the solitary, old bachelor-curmudgeon, the grave-digger Gabriel Grub, is the prototype, or first version, of Ebenezer Scrooge."

Did he work behind the picture house?

"Ah, so that's the local connection you seek. Dickens often stayed at the Talbot Hotel and a certain acquaintance worked as an accountant in chambers behind what we know as the Palace Cinema, but back in the 1840s it was the Corn Exchange and only became a theatre in 1914. The office building still stands. Apparently Dickens drew on the appearance of the office there for the tank in which Scrooge and his clerk Bob Cratchit worked. The remainder of the setting came from the author's childhood in Camden Town, which had unseasonably cold Christmases from 1812 to 1820. However, Charles Dickens had no more nor fewer white Christmases than you or I can expect here in Old Malton."

The clock struck nine and our Jimmy came back and climbed onto the settee, still wiping his mouth. His eyes were all red.

"Er, mister Fenwick," he said, "yer dog's been sick." But the old man didn't hear him. Shurrup, I said, say nowt and let him get on. Fenwick had some bloomin' good batteries in tonight, he just kept going.

"Dickens has been accused of romanticizing the foibles of the industrial revolution," You what? I said. "Well, most of the working class people were very poor in those days," he said.

"Mam says we're poor," said Jimmy. No she doesn't, I said, giving him a kick, She says we're not very well off, and that's different.

"Yes," said Mr Fenwick, "Indeed it is. Wealth is a broad category."

See, me Dad said Scrooge comes from Malton, that's what Mam needs to know.

"Yes, quite," said Fenwick, looking at Mam's note again. "But I'm afraid he's incorrect. Your father didn't attend school in Malton, did he?" No, I said, he's from Pickering.

Fenwick, nodded slowly, as if that accounted for a lot. Mam always says it does.

"To summarize, then, please remind your mother, and inform your father, that neither Dickens nor his fictitious character Ebenezer Scrooge came from Malton. The office depicted in *A Christmas Carol*, however, can be said to have been conceived in this town, as you suggest. Another point of local interest is that Jacob Marley's name was derived from our local term for soil: *marl*. It's also the term that some of our hill farmers use for sleet."

Right you are then, thank-you, I said. We'll be away now. We got off the settee and went back down the gloomy passage, Fenwick leading the way with the lamp. Then it dawned on me, there was no electric in this house. I bet he's never even seen Scrooge on the telly.

He opened the door to let us out, but he kept his dog in. So, I said, Scrooge wasn't from Malton but his office was.

"Yes, well, I suppose you could say that," he said, "Goodnight, boys, and a Merry Christmas to you and your family."

Goodnight, I said, Merry Christmas.

"Ey, do you want a carol?" said Jimmy, but he'd shut the door.

We ran back down Cemetery Lane, and didn't save the torch batteries. When we got home Dad was in his armchair reading the *Radio Times* and Mam was sat on some newspaper on the floor, polishing some brass candlesticks.

"So," she said, "how's Mr Fenwick?"

"He's bloomin' old," said Jimmy.

"Yes, love, and what did he have to say?" Scrooge isn't from Malton he's from *Pickwick Papers*, I said.

"And that Jacob Marley's from a farm round here where it sleets a lot," said Jimmy.

"And the office," said Dad, "Scrooge's office, where's that from?"

Malton, me and Jimmy said, both together.

"See, just like I told your mother," said Dad and he slapped his leg with the *Radio Times*.

Mam dropped a candlestick, looked at the ceiling and said summat about God giving her strength. I thought about the film again. Ey, Mam, I said, where does the Ghost of Christmas Yet to Come, come from?

"Oh," she says, "you mean the scary one that dresses funny, with mean-looking hands and he never says anything nice?" Aye, that one.

"I'll bet he's from Pickering," she said.

6

Buried Treasure

I never meant to go looking for ought. Honest. I was being good. I just happened to be in me Mam and Dad's bedroom. Doin' nowt. Near the wardrobe.

Y'see, I still believe in Father Christmas, but I knew he didn't bring *all* the presents on Christmas Eve. I'd seen a few of 'em come in through the back door, with neighbours and me aunts and uncles. They smuggled a few presents in for him. All that whisperin'. I knew.

Me Mam thought I hadn't noticed but I had. I sometimes think she thinks I'm daft, sometimes. But I aren't.

Some of our presents came ages before Christmas, but most of 'em came just a few days before. Folks'd come in with a big shopping bag and sit down in the kitchen. Mam would make 'em a cup o'tea if it was a woman, or pour 'em a drop o'Lambs Navy Rum if it was a man. Then she'd send me off somewhere to do summat, like fetch some onions from the wash house. When I got back the shopping bag would be empty and they'd suddenly start talking about the price of eggs. I'm not that stupid.

So, somewhere in our house, right this minute, was a load of presents. All wrapped and ready. Hidden. Waiting for Christmas Day. Well, I couldn't wait. I mean, Christmas Day was ages away yet. Two full days and nights.

Anyway, I'd been all through the cupboard under the stairs and found nowt but the usual rubbish. There was nothing in the airing cupboard but vests, and underpants and socks, and the big bin at the back of the pantry just had some taties in with long white roots growing out of 'em.

It would be daft to hide Christmas presents in our bedroom, and I don't think they'd leave 'em outside in the coalhouse or the shed. So that only left Mam and Dad's bedroom. Aye, well, here I was then. Just having a quick look. No 'arm in that.

I found some fluff and a green sock under their bed, and the jerry o'course, but I kept well clear o'that. And all the chest of drawers was full of Mam's clothes. Nowt under the dressing table and I did find a *Marks and Spencers* bag behind the curtains, but there was just a nightie in it. New. It must be going back.

The wardrobe was the last place to look. I wasn't supposed to go in there. I wasn't supposed to even be in Mam and Dad's bedroom, unless I was bringing Dad a cup o'tea or summat, and he wasn't home yet. Mam was in the kitchen peelin' some taties for the tea so she'd be down there for a bit. No idea where our Jimmy was.

I went over to the wardrobe, and stood on that bloomin' squeaky floorboard. I stopped and listened to see if Mam had heard. She hadn't, so I reached for the wardrobe door and turned the little handle. There was a loud *click*, Damn! I bet she heard that...and I waited, holding me breath, but she was still singing along to summat on the wireless so I knew she hadn't.

I slowly pulled the door open and got that wardrobe smell of moth balls, and dresses, and Mam's perfume and Dad's best boots, all mixed up in me face. It was about full in there, with jackets and frocks and cardigans all hung from coat hangers.

And down at the bottom there'd be nowt but shoes, but then I noticed a brown blanket. All across the bottom where the shoes should be. I pulled a corner of it up and had a look. Like I thought, there was some shoes, but on top of 'em were lots of parcels, most of 'em done up with red Christmas paper. One or two were in brown paper, a couple in silver paper, and there was one in just newspaper. Bingo! *Presents!*

I knelt down and picked one up. It was heavy and when I shook it there was a clumping noise, like... like a pair of boots in a box. I looked for the label. To Jimmy, with Love, it said. So, Jimmy was getting some boots. Now then, where's all my stuff... I picked up another box and gave it a rattle. It sounded like a jam-jar full o'gravel. Either that or whatever it was had bust. I put it back and picked up another.

It was great, trying to guess what was in 'em all. Some were real heavy and some were light, like they had nowt in 'em. I was just reaching into the far corner for a big 'un when suddenly a hand grabbed me neck. Argh! I've been caught!

"What yer doing in there, Der?" It was our Jimmy, whispering, cos he knew just how stupid it was to get caught in here. Nowt, I said, shurrup, I'm just looking at stuff. Me 'eart was thumping like 'ell now.

"Let me see," he said, and he shoved his way in, standing right on a big flat box wrapped in silver paper. He still had his shoes on and the box gave way. Yer great gawp! I said, Yer squashing stuff, gerrout!

"What stuff, Der? What's in there?" Presents, yer daft beggar, I said, Christmas presents!

" 'As he been already, then, Father Christmas, as he been? He's a bit bloomin' early, eh?" No, I said, It's stuff other people have brought. Mam and Dad must hide 'em all in here while Christmas Eve and then...

"Or maybe Father Christmas hides 'em in here, to save him time on Christmas Eve. Maybe he drops a few off when he's coming past on t'way to Malton." Shurrup, I said, I don't think it's him that hides 'em. I've seen people bring 'em to the house, and then... and then I heard somebody coming upstairs. Oh no. Quick! I said, gerrin, and shurrup.

We both jammed into the back of the wardrobe and I pulled the door closed behind us. It was dark, and the smell of clothes and perfume and shoes and stuff was like a great big blanket smothering me.

I don't like being in small places. I hate it. Can't breathe. Me Mam says I'm clostophonic, like she is. But I daren't scream. And now there was another smell anorl. Ey, I said to Jimmy, have you stepped in some dog muck?

He was holding on to me belt, frightened to death, as if he'd fall down a big hole somewhere. Shh!, I said. Quiet. He moved his foot and I could hear a squishing sound. Like when the last of the Fairy Liquid comes out of the bottle.

Whoever it was came into the bedroom, muttering summat about fried eggs and no sausages. It was me Dad. He sat on the bed, and I heard it creak, then I heard his shoes come off and drop to the floor. Thud, one. Thud, two. He'd be getting changed. Shirt off, now his trousers. Then I could hear him scratching. He does this a lot after work. He says it's the sawdust. Mam says it's cos he's like a monkey.

Then he had a good stretch and we could hear him groan... *hmmmmoooer*. Then he let off! Real loud. A real buck snorter. It was too much for our Jimmy who bust out laughing. Shh! I said, quiet, but it was too late. I heard the squeaky floorboard go then the wardrobe door flew open, and me Dad pulled back the stuff on the hangers and stood there in his droopy underpants, looking down at us.

"What the 'ell are you doin' in there? Eh?" We were... er, we were playing hide and seek, I said.

"Oh aye," says Dad, "and who's doing the bloody seeking then, since yer both hiding?" Oh no. That was daft. I hadn't thought o'that. Me brother had, though, sorta.

"Er, we weren't sure whose turn it was to hide," said Jimmy, "so we both did." Really?

I thought we might get a belt, but me Dad was standing there in just his socks and underpants so maybe he wouldn't feel like it.

"Come on, get out o'there and get down them stairs sharpish, before I box yer lugs." We fell out of the wardrobe and shot through the bedroom door. Not even a tap on the backside. I knew he was looking too daft to do ought and probably wanted to get some clothes on cos it's always freezin' upstairs.

Mind, if he told Mam where we'd been we were good as dead. And I hadn't forgotten about Jimmy's shoes and what they might have wiped off on them presents.

Funny thing was, we just sat and had our teas, and nobody said owt. On Christmas Eve I didn't tell Jimmy what he was getting, or what it felt like he was getting, but when he started going on and on about wanting a cowboy outfit with white holsters and a hat and a silver badge, and them chaps they wear with fringes on... I felt like saying, aye well t'only cowboy outfit you're getting is a pair of 'obnail boots from Yates' so you'll just have to mosey on down to t'coral in them buggers.

On Christmas morning, we grabbed our pillow cases, full o'presents, from the end of the bed and went downstairs and sat on the settee, ready to take turns opening 'em, like we always do. Mam had her tidy little pile of presents near her chair, and Dad had his on the rug in front of the telly. There was a rotten smell coming out of my pillowcase and Mam and Dad kept looking at each other. Dad coughed.

Mam went first, and opened her present from Aunt Judy. We all leaned over to have a good look, cos that what we do in our family. Whenever anybody opens a present we crowd round 'em and make a bit o'fuss. It was me Mam's idea I think.

She's annoying is me Mam, cos she takes ages opening owt. She tries to undo the Sellotape, and everybody know you can't, then she unfolds the paper one bit at a time. It's like watching one o'them things on telly that goes backwards. You start off with a Christmas present and end up with a big sheet of wrapping paper, some folded ribbon, some bits o'used Sellotape, and whatever was wrapped up in it. Hardly a surprise.

The present turned out to be a load of smelly stuff for in the bath. Except that it had all got mixed up. A bit squashed. Well, the bubble bath had leaked all over the bath salts and the soap had broken in half. But it was all bonny colours.

Mum looked a bit upset. "Oh dear, love," said me Dad, "Old Father Christmas must have had a bit of squeeze on gerrin down our chimney this year."

"Aye, 'appen," said Mam, "and I wonder how he got on with that box of Black Magic you asked him for." Oh no, I hope bloomin' Jimmy hadn't stood on that anorl! Dad was crackers over Black Magic chocolates and he always got one of them big boxes, every year.

Me Dad opened a packet of hankies that had his initials sewn on, and he started testing 'em all, real loud, until Mam slapped his leg and told him not to be so vulgar.

Our Jimmy went next and opened his big box. The boots, I thought. We all leaned over to see. Yeah, boots. They were black and shiny, with real big treads on the bottom.

"By go," said Dad, "Them'll hold some cow muck on the bottom, Jim!" And Mam slapped him again.

Jimmy started to thread the boots with long laces that came with 'em, while I pulled out me big present, the one in silver paper.

The paper was a bit torn and I could see a cardboard box underneath with some coloured letters. *Istry*, it said. Oh no, I thought, not a bloomin' 'istory game. Me Mam likes 'istory but I can't stand it. But when I got all the paper off I could see that it said *Chemistry*. It was a chemistry set, and it didn't half stink. The box was dented in and the picture on the front, of a young lass in a white jacket thing, looked all blotchy. I took the lid off and the smell of dog muck came up and just about choked me.

"Good grief!" said me Dad, "What's that Father Christmas brought you, last week's fish guts?"

"Ron!" said me Mam, though I could see she didn't like the smell either. And neither of 'em leaned over to have a closer look.

"Whoa, that's alright, Der," said our Jimmy, then he went back to lacing up his new boots.

There was a lot of little test tubes, and some of 'em were bust. And a lot of little packets of stuff, white stuff, black stuff, green stuff, red stuff, orange stuff... all scattered about. Some of 'em mixed together and most of 'em making that bloody awful stink.

Me Dad leaned across and picked up one of the packets. "Iron filings," he said, "ey, I'll show you a trick." And he poured some out into his hand, shouted "*Alla kazam*!"and threw 'em all on t'fire. There was a bit of a whoosh and a lot o'sparks went flying up t'chimney and a Christmas card fell off the mantlepiece.

"Heh heh, look you there," Dad said, "Me uncle Gordon taught me how to do that at t'blacksmith's shop."

"I wish he'd taught you summat useful," said Mam, picking up the card, "like how to read."

"Gi's a go, Der," said Jimmy, "c'on, gi's a go!" But I already had the rest of the packet poured out into me hand and I threw it at the fireplace. *WHOOSH!* It went, and the rest of the Christmas cards fell off the mantlepiece.

"Bloody 'ell, steady on lad!" Dad said, and me Mam started picking the cards up real quick and saying summat about it being a stupid idea, just like she said it was in the shop. Then she stopped and looked at me.

"I meant the workshop, love, where Father Christmas makes all his toys."

Usually, when me Mam looks right at me like this, I look at me feet, or the kitchen wall, or at summat I've just picked out of me pocket, or me nose... but this time I looked right back at her. In the eyes. She was waiting for me to say summat. I think she was waiting for me to own up, to say that I'd been into their bedroom and looked in the wardrobe, and found all these presents, and that I knew Father Christmas hadn't really brought 'em. But he had, some of 'em. And Jimmy didn't need to know so he can still believe in Father Christmas. And I believe in Father Christmas.

I wanted to say sorry but I couldn't. So I said nowt, then I gave Mam me bar of fruit and nut chocolate I'd got from Chalky White's missus, same as she got Jimmy, and said it was her turn to open.

We went round and round opening stuff, until there was nowt left to open, and sat there with our presents, a lot of 'em squashed or broken, and this bloody awful smell still hanging about everywhere.

Jimmy had his new boots on and was marching about, squashing down all the piles of wrapping paper. Dad was poking around in his Black Magic, eating three at a time cos that's how they came out of the box, all squished together. Mam was reading a cookbook on pickling she'd got from Granny.

"Why are half the presents all flattened and bashed up, Mam?" said Jimmy.

"I don't know, love" she said. "Maybe Father Christmas has to be a bit more careful about where he keeps 'em in future," and she looked at me Dad, but he didn't say owt. He just offered her a coffee creme. Well, half of one. Next year, I thought, as well as sending him a letter up the chimney, I'm going to leave a note inside Mam and Dad's wardrobe saying *Hey, don't be leaving presents in here! Keep 'em safe while Christmas.*

Maybe Mam didn't know that he'd hidden 'em in the wardrobe. Maybe she thought he'd been clumsy coming down the chimney, or fallen on his sack. I didn't want her to be thinking it was his fault. Or maybe she thought I'd stepped on 'em all and squashed 'em. But I hadn't. It wasn't fair! I hadn't! Suddenly I was shouting out loud. *It wasn't me, Mam, I didn't stand on the presents! Honest, it wasn't me... it... it was our Jimmy!*

Jimmy kicked me with his new boots, hard, but Mam didn't say owt. And Dad never even looked up from his Black Magic.

"You don't half talk rubbish, our Derek," he said. "Here, 'ave a squished marzipan. Merry Christmas."

7

Wassail!

There was nowt wrong with Christmas, as far as I was concerned. But Mam had been on about it getting too commercial, whatever that means.

"People seem to have forgotten what it's all about," she said one teatime while we were having our beans on toast. "All they seem to care about is spend spend spend, and it doesn't grow on trees y'know."

I'd 'eard her talk like this before. We all had. It was usually about birthdays, though, or holidays, or new television sets or summat. But not Christmas. Anyway, it was always to do with money. Or with us not having any.

"Aye, love, I think you're right," said Dad, and at first I couldn't believe that he was actually agreeing with her. Whatever it was, it was bloomin' serious. Our Jimmy piped up.

"What do you mean, Dad?"

"Well, son," he said, wiping the last of the beans off his plate with some crust, "What I mean is that people these days just want more and more stuff at Christmas."

I couldn't see ought wrong with that, so count me in with the people on this one.

"They seem to think you can just buy yourself a good Christmas by getting more and more decorations, more presents, more clothes, and more food..." I notice he didn't say more drink.

"Yes, that's just what I mean," said Mam, pouring tea into our mugs and taking the top off the biscuit tin. "We never had a lot o'stuff at Christmas when I was a girl."

"No," said Dad, "just an orange in your stocking, and maybe a few monkey nuts."

"And a piece of coal," said Mam, "washed, of course."

"Aye, that's right, a lump o'coal for good luck."

Here we go, I thought, he'll be telling us about sending small boys up chimneys next, and walkin' ten miles to school and back with no shoes in twenty-foot o'snow, uphill both ways. He often says that.

"It was Christmas spirit that mattered," he said, "not the presents."

"Good job anorl if it was just a bloomin' orange," said our Jimmy, but they ignored him.

After tea we all sat in the front room cos it was freezin' everywhere else. They were still talking about the old days and Christmas spirit, and I knew our Jimmy thought it was something you got from the pub, cos I'd read him that little sign above the door a fair few times. See, me Dad used to be real proud that I could read a bit before a lot of other kids, so he'd show me off to his mates at the pub by getting me to read the little black sign above the pub door, the one that said *Arthur Smith, licensed to sell beer, wine and spirits for consumption on or off the premises*. I had a bit o'bother with the word *consumption* at first.

Anyway, our telly was bust again so they sat and looked into the fire while me and Jimmy lay on the hearthrug with our comics.

"We used to make all our Christmas presents," said Mam. "We'd knit socks and gloves and tea cosies, and make jam and chutney and dress up the jars with little bits of red gingham fabric, tied with ribbon..."

"We should do that again," said Dad.

"We?" said Mam. "When did you learn to knit? And if you think I'm letting you loose in that kitchen with a hotplate and me good pans you've another think coming."

"Be cheaper than shopping," he said, "and I can do ribbons, I'm good wi'knots." He sniffed.

"No. Electric train sets, new bikes, dolls that wet themselves... that's not what they were thinking about when they came up with Christmas," said Mam. Who's they? I said. Who invented Christmas, Mam?

"Christmas was invented, if you want to call it that, in York, actually."

"You what?" said me Dad. "I know we've come up with some champion stuff in Yorkshire but I didn't think Christmas was our idea."

Me Mam sat up straight, and put on her Grammar School voice. "It was back in King Arthur's day. He'd kicked out the Saxons in the year 520 A.D. and then he went up north, but his bishops asked him not to kill the Scots because they'd just got hold of the bible, and it wasn't on for Christians to go round killing other Christians."

She looked at me and Jimmy to make sure we were listening. At times like this she thought we might learn summat.

"So, on his way back from Scotland, Arthur had a big meeting with all his clergy in York, more like a party really, and they celebrated the first ever Christmas in Britain."

"Well, I'll go to t'back of our coalhouse!" said me Dad, "Is that right?"

"Yes," said Mam, "It is. Holidays, or holy days, were always welcome back then, and a big celebration pulls folk together, makes them forget about killing each other for a bit. Religion seemed like a good excuse at the time. Mind, a lot of people think Jesus was born in September... and King William the Conqueror was crowned on Christmas Day in 1066. It was political, really. See, when your peasants are busy feasting and drinking they're a lot easier to keep an eye on."

"How come a woman like you who's so good at history can't remember where she's left her handbag?" said Dad, but Mam kept talking.

"There's been all sorts of Christmas customs through the years. Some we've forgotten and some we've kept, and maybe changed a bit."

"Football at Scarborough," said me Dad. "Aye, there's allus a football match on Scarborough sands at Christmas, lads, between the firemen and the stokers, or there was. Me Grandad was from Scarborough and he used to play. Y'see lads, it was because there was a real bad storm back in 1863,"

"1893," said Mam.

"Like I said, in 1893, twenty fishing boats were out in a real bad storm and folks in town waited and waited, and they all got safely back to harbour, all except one, a boat called *The Evelyn and Michael*,"

"*Evelyn and Maud*," said Mam.

"*Evelyn and Maud*," said Dad, "and so they all got together and had a football match on the sands to raise money for the families. Fishermen versus firemen, but not them firemen that ride on fire engines, I mean the firemen that used to shovel coal to keep the furnace fires going, cos they were steamboats back then, y'see. Any road, the firemen won first year, four nil, and they raised ninety pounds..."

"Nine pounds," said Mam.

"For charity. And every year since they've played football on t'sands. Me Grandad used to take me when I was your age. Every Christmas Day."

"Except now it's on Boxing Day," said Mam.

"Why's it called Boxing Day?" said Jimmy.

"Cos that's when we box yer lugs for nagging!" and me Dad pretended to clip our Jimmy's ear.

"No, love," said Mam, "It's because when people went to church at Christmas they used to put some money in a wooden box, for charity. Next day, December 26, they'd open the box and share it out among the poor of the parish."

Jimmy said we should go to church on Boxing Day and see if we could get some.

"There were yule logs, and mummers..."

"Hey, remember Wassailing?" said Dad, "*Here we come a-wassailing among the leaves so green, here we come a-wandering so...* er... summat... *to be seen*,"

"Fair," said Mam.

"*Our wassail cup is made of...* er, whatisit..."

"The rosemary tree."

"*And so is your beer of the best barley, call up the butler of this house, put on his...* er, thingummy bob,"

"Golden ring."

"*And let him bring us a glass of beer for the better we shall sing...*"

What you on about, Dad?

"It's what they used to do, lad, to spread Christmas cheer around the village. They'd have a big Wassail cup and fill it with good stuff to drink, then go round the houses making toasts and singing."

"Ey, can we have a go?" said Jimmy.

"You certainly can't!" said Mam.

"Aw, come on lass, you said you liked the old ways o'Christmas."

Me Mam just looked at him, the way she does when she wants to say no but can't be bothered to argue, so she breathes out instead and everybody knows that means yes.

Have we got one o'them Wassail cups, Dad?

"You know summat, lad, I think we 'appen do," and he went diving into the cupboard under the stairs, flinging wellies and old shopping baskets out behind him and singing the Wassailing song, or the bits he could remember. Mam just sat shaking her head and looking at the telly, wishing it wasn't bust.

"Here we are!" he said and came across on his knees carrying a blue and white jug sorta thing, with two handles on it. "I'd forgotten about this," he said.

"Aye," said Mam, "and it should maybe stay forgotten anorl. And one o'them handles is cracked."

"It's the real McCoy is this," he said, "Me granny had this on her sideboard for years, with hydrangeas in it."

"Hyacinths, yer daft 'apeth," said Mam.

"Right lads, quick rinse out and we'll fettle it for Wassailing!" We followed him into the kitchen.

"What we gonna drink out of it, Dad?" said Jimmy, and I was wondering anorl, cos there was no lemonade left and I'd finished the orange juice at teatime.

Mam was shouting from the front room, summat about no booze for them lads, but Dad wasn't listening. He went into the corner cupboard and brought out a couple of bottles. Some sherry and summat else with two dogs on the label. Then he reached up behind some tins in the pantry and came out with a bottle of cherry brandy.

"Right, this'll do it," he said, and poured a drop from each bottle into the jug, going round and round, a drop more from each, cos it was a big jug, until the bottles were all empty.

He lifted the jug, had a sniff and then a taste. "By gum!" he said, "That's right stuff! A bit sweet, maybe," and he looked around for summat else to put in.

"There's some milk here, Dad," said Jimmy.

"Ooh no, son, not milk..." I passed him the teapot, still half full from teatime, but a bit cold now.

"Heh, good idea, Derek, why not?" he said, and poured the rest of it into the Wassail jug. I saw some tea leaves go in but I didn't say anything, I just wanted to get going. I opened the back door, so Dad could take the empty bottles out to the dustbin, before Mam saw 'em, and when I turned round I saw Jimmy putting the top back on the cough syrup. He likes Delrosa, does Jimmy, and Mam usually keeps it hidden, so I don't know where it came from. It was a big bottle but there was nowt left in it now.

61

When Dad finally decided the Wassail cup was full enough to share round the village, he told us to put our coats and wellies on. Before we set off we went into the front room to show Mam. Dad thought he might still persuade her to come and join us. He was wrong.

"Right, love, we're off Wassailing," said me Dad, holding up the jug with both hands, "are you sure you aren't coming? It'll be a right laugh."

"Aye, it probably will," she said, "for all the wrong reasons. No I am not coming," she said, "parading round the streets with that thing, what does it look like?"

"Looks like there'll be just three of us," said Dad. "Come on, lads, let's be out there!" And we said goodbye to Mam and went out the back door. It was a cold night so I knew Jimmy was going to be moaning. Especially since I couldn't find my gloves so I'd borrowed his.

"Right lads, we'll do Chalky White first, next door but one." I wondered why he didn't do Mrs Blenkin right next door to us first, cos she'd like a Wassail to cheer her up, she was always so miserable. We cut across her flower beds and went up to Chalky's door. Dad knocked.

"*Here we come a-Wassailing among the leaves so green, here we come...* sing up, lads!" And me and Jimmy sang Here we come a-Wassailing among the leaves so green, but Dad was doing the second part by then. It sounded a bit like when we do the *London's Burning* song in class and take turns to start off, but it sounded a lot worse. Dad sang the first line again and tried to catch us up before we got to the rosemary tree, then the front door opened and Chalky White stood there looking as if he'd seen a ghost, or summat worse.

"Ey up, Chalky," said Dad, "we wish you Wassail, don't we lads." Yeah, we said, *Wassail!*

"Wass what?" said Chalky, scratching his bum with one hand and his head with the other.

"Wassail," said Dad, "It's what they used to say before merry Christmas. Cheers!" and he took a big drink from the jug then held it out.

"Oh, aye," said Chalky, still scratching with one hand but holding the other out to the jug, "what you supping there? Wass ale? Who brews that then?"

"No, it's not ale like at t'pub, it's Wassail. It's traditional, all sorts o'stuff, more like a, er, cocktail I suppose, aye, an old-fashioned Christmas cocktail. It's grand in't'it lads," and he let me and Jimmy have a drink, maybe to show that it wasn't poison. Mind, it tasted like poison. I spit mine back in.

"Nay, Ron, ta very much, but I don't drink cocktails, me. Hey but I've known the wife to have a martini at Christmas, 'ang on." And he turned round and shouted, "Mother, get yerself out here, Ron Bradley's got some Christmas cocktail in a jug."

I was wondering if we got money for doing the Wassail song, like you do for carol singing, but Dad never said ought about that. Mrs Chalky came to the door, wiping her hands on a tea towel. She had white stuff all down her pinny and her face was red.

"Phew, goodness me. Just doing me Christmas baking, it's like an oven is our back kitchen," she said, "I'm right parched."

"Wassail then," said Dad, and held the jug to her mouth, "this'll fettle you!" and she took a big gulp. She didn't have much option since the handle with the crack suddenly broke off and the jug slipped and the wassail stuff all slopped into her face. It went up her nose and in her eyes and a fair bit disappeared into her mouth. She started to snort like a pig and cough.

"Ey up lass, steady on!" said Chalky, you're supposed to just sip these cocktail things." He grabbed the tea towel and wiped her face, leaving bits o'pastry on her cheeks and her eyebrows.

She didn't seem very happy. Dad was trying to stick the handle back on, but without any glue. It didn't work, so he put it in his pocket. Apart from all her coughing it was very quiet. Somebody ought to say summat, I thought. *Wassail!* Mrs White, I said.

"Aye, *Wassail*!" shouted Jimmy.

"Is she alright?" said Dad. "She supped a fair drop..."

"Aye, she's grand," said Chalky, "but I'll get her onto t'settee for a bit. Can you shut t'door after me."

And he put her arm over his shoulder and sort of carried her back into the house, like cowboys carry their mates when they've been shot.

"Er, Wassail, then, er, Chalky," said Dad, quietly, as he pulled the door closed. Me and Jimmy looked at each other. The Wassail stuff tasted bloomin' awful but it didn't half make you feel warm. Jimmy had stopped moaning about his hands being cold.

Where we off next, Dad?

"Right then, let's see..." and he looked up and down the street. "Ah know, Snack Waudby's, he'll be in right fettle for a Wassail."

But when we got there he wasn't. Snack Waudby just laughed while Dad showed him how to drink from the jug. He asked what was in it but Dad said he couldn't rightly remember. Then Snack went and brought old Granny Waudby to the door, and she just laughed anorl.

Summat similar happened at the next house, and the next one, and about three after that. Since we had no takers Dad was the only one drinking Wassail. He was full of old-fashioned Christmas spirit, though, and he wasn't ready to pack in.

"Alright lads, we'll do Westgate," he said, "while we still have a decent drop left." And we set off for Woody's shop corner, walking real fast.

He'd got the hang of the Wassail song by now. Well, the first verse, anyway, and he was singing it real loud.

He was up in front and just as he reached the corner he turned back to say "Come on, lads, 'urry up!" And that's when he slipped.

It might have been some dog muck, or it might have been his shoelace that had been undone all night. He would have gone full length, anorl, if it hadn't been for Copper Wiggle.

Constable Wiggle is the village bobby, and he was coming round the corner the other way, pushing his bike. Now, I remember somebody once telling me that when a policeman hasn't got his hat on it means he's not on duty. And Copper Wiggle's hat was on the ground now, in a sticky puddle of Wassail.

His big black policeman's bike was lying across the top of Dad, who still had the last handle of the jug in his hand, but nowt else, and the bike's wheel was still going round... *tick-tick-tick, tick-tick-tick, tick-tick-tick...*

I thought about running away, but then I thought I saw something real interesting in Woody's shop window and I pulled our Jimmy over to see it. Out of the way, keep us heads down, like, as if we weren't there. It were all Dad's idea so if there was going to be any trouble it was all Dad's fault.

"Mr Bradley?" said Constable Wiggle. He sounded real cross. "What *have* you got to say for yourself?"

It was fairly obvious what he had to say, really. "Wassail, Copper," he said, "*Wassail!*"

8

The Bow

I remember waking up early that Saturday morning. It was cold, and it felt grey. It was always cold and grey in our bedroom and you could never tell if it was raining or snowing or foggy or what cos the window always looked the same, wet grey, until you gave it a wipe.

I was just going to get our Jimmy to go and wipe it with his sleeve when he jumped onto my bed. "Three more sleeps!" he shouted, "Just three more sleeps!" Get lost, I said, and pushed him off. He crashed onto the floor and just missed the jerry by inches. He wasn't bleeding but I knew he'd cry, and then we heard "*QUIET* you lads!"

It was me Dad, downstairs. See! I said, you've got him in a bad mood already and he hasn't even seen yer bloomin' face yet this morning. Jimmy just sniffed, cos he knew he couldn't cry now or he'd be even more in trouble. And he'd take me with him. "Well you just leave me alone then," he said, "or we won't get to go."

We had to be good today. Very good. It was the last Saturday before Christmas. Christmas shopping day. We would all walk into Malton with about two shopping bags each and Mam and Dad would buy everything we needed for Christmas. Some dates, some nuts for in that bowl, a bottle of Bristol Cream sherry that tasted nowt like cream, some Babychams for Mam and a lot of pairs of socks and gloves for people. That was the boring bit. But we'd also get to go to the CO-OP and sit on Father Christmas' knee and tell him what we wanted for Christmas. That was the good bit.

Some of the other kids in school had been asking if I still believed in Father Christmas, as though one of these years belief would just run out. Like money, or coal. Well, to be honest, and I haven't told anybody this so you be quiet when you've heard it. I think I do believe, but I'm not stupid. I mean I know he doesn't come down the chimney with all the presents and stuff cos you've only got to stick your head round the fireplace and yer black, and he never looks black in the pictures. And I think all that stuff about the reindeer's a bit far-fetched. Look, I have thought about it, a lot, but I don't know how he gets here or into the house, and I don't much care, as long as he comes. And I know that if he really was complete magic and made absolutely anything you wanted, then I'd get whatever I asked for, and I never did.

Every year Dad would say "Father Christmas isn't made o'money you know!"

Then Mam would say "Well, you know he might not be able to bring you all that this year." So I don't know if parents pay him for making presents, or if they give him some money to go out and buy stuff, but somewhere along the line there seems to be a limit on what you can actually get from him. And I don't know why Mam always says "We can't afford it," if it's up to Father Christmas, not her.

Mind, as me Dad says, it doesn't hurt to ask. And it seems you can still ask for whatever you want because when you get on Father Christmas' knee in the CO-OP the mams and dads are usually miles away buying gloves and socks. See, I think that when you stop believin' then that's when you start getting all the boring presents bought for you by relatives. Boring relatives always get you boring stuff. So I think it's worth believin'. And it doesn't cost owt.

Anyway, when we got to Malton this morning I was going to ask Father Christmas for a bow and arrow for Christmas, a real one, not one of them daft little things with a rubber sucker on the end that you have to spit on so they stick. No, I wanted a real bow and real arrows, like Robin Hood's but more modern, with steel tips that could stick into trees and coalhouse doors, and maybe, if I went off across the fields real quiet, a rabbit. I could be a hunter! I could go hunting and bring all kinds of game home for a feast.

A real bow would make me a real hunter. And I knew I couldn't have a gun like Grandad's cos I'd been asking for that every bloomin' year.

So, I had it all planned out what I'd ask for when we went to the CO-OP. That was a good bit of the day, and then we'd go for our dinners in a cafe somewhere, and that was another good bit.

Me Dad was opening the back door. "Are you lads ready then or what?" So we pulled our good clothes on and ran downstairs. Well, I ran but Jimmy seemed to trip near the top step, just as he was trying to get in front of me, but anyway we both got down and he soon stopped cryin' when Dad threatened to leave him behind.

Here, eat this on the way, I don't want you two natterin' for grub as soon as we get there." And Mam gave us both a thick slice o'toast with strawberry jam on.

I knew there was Christmas magic in the air cos we both found our coats and wellies first go and without being shouted at. Two minutes later we were off, carrying our empty bags, marching up the street towards Malton.

Me and Jimmy walked in front and kicked through the leaves while Mam and Dad walked a bit behind, talking quietly, like they do when somebody's died or when they don't want us to hear. I didn't care, it would soon be my turn to talk quietly and have a secret, when I saw Father Christmas on me own, to have a quiet word, as me Dad would say.

The shopping was boring as usual. Dad argued with the butcher about the turkey and Mam went red and left the shop, dragging us with her. We piled into the greengrocer's and loaded about fifteen bags full of spuds and onions and stuff.

I asked for some holly with bright red berries on but Dad said buying it was stupid, cos he could get some for nowt. Mam told him to shush then smiled nicely at the man behind the counter.

Outside, after she'd said her usual bit about never having been so embarrassed, though we all know she has been, we set off down the main street to the CO-OP. Dad was laughing, in between singing "*Oh, the Holly and the ivy, when they are both full grown, of all the trees that are in the wood it's the holly that gets nicked.*" Me Mam said he was showing her up and kept shushing him.

Then we were there, at the CO-OP doorway. There was tinsel round the doorway, well, most of it. A bit was coming off and dangling down, and hittin' peoples' heads as they walked in. Tall people, anyway. We went in. I could see him right away, down a long passage between some settees and tables, up on a platform thing covered in pretend snow with a little house behind him. He was on a big red chair and just in front of him was an Elf, in a pointy red hat, a short green coat and glasses. She looked just like Jane Ibbotson who used to live opposite but moved when she turned sixteen last year. Just like her.

"Now then Jane," said me Mam to the Elf as we got to the front, "Just keep an eye on these two, we'll be back in ten minutes, just going upstairs to clothing, alright?"

"Right lads," said the Elf, "Want to see Father Christmas do ya? Just stand there," she said, and pulled a bit of rope around behind us, as if we were going to turn round and run off or summat. "You'll have to wait a minute til he's finished with Tommy Fletcher, and you won't have long cos it's about time for his dinner."

Tommy Fletcher, now there's a smarmy little beggar if you ever had to shoot one. Teacher's pet. And he was taking bloomin' ages to ask for his presents. He was reading from a flippin' list and I thought that was a bit off but the Elf didn't seem to mind and Father Christmas didn't say ought either, but he looked at his watch twice.

Then it was us. I stepped up but then felt a pull on me collar that nearly put me bloomin' neck out.

"Jimmy first, he's youngest," said the Elf, and she pushed him through and up to Father Christmas. He was looking tired, and when Jimmy climbed up on his knee he made a noise like me Grandad sometimes does, like a balloon going down real slow.

He had some black glasses on, round they were, but they were mended in the middle with Sellotape. His beard wasn't very white either, and it looked a lot like cotton wool, but I'm sure it was really him.

The Elf came over and leant down to me. "So, what do you want for Christmas then, Derek? Eh?" She was making me turn around so I couldn't listen in on what our Jimmy asking for. I thought, I'm not telling her, what's it got to do with her? She's just an Elf. Sod you, I'm only telling Father Christmas. A quiet word.

"Come on," she said, "let's be knowing what you want. If you don't tell us you might end up getting nowt." But I just want to tell Father Christmas, not you.

"Oh don't be so daft," she said, "I end up telling him anyway cos he forgets everything. You don't want him forgetting what you ask for do you? You might end up with a hoola hoop."

Aw no! Who wants a flippin' hoola hoop? Well, I said, actually I'd like a bow and arrow. A real one. Not with a rubber sucker on the end but with steel tips that'll stick in...

"Oh, a bow and arrow, eh?" she said. "Right, I'll tell him," and then she unclipped her bit of rope again and pushed me back through, away from Father Christmas.

I looked round but he was getting up off his big red chair now and Jimmy was coming back to me, all smiling and daft looking, and he had a red lollipop anorl.

Hey where'd ya get that? I said, and he just nodded behind.

"Him, he's gorra bag full." And I looked but Father Christmas had gone, and the Elf was across talking to a woman near the table lamps. She'd stuck a sign on the rope saying *Back at One*. I never got to see him! It wasn't bloomin' fair!

"So I asked him for a train," said our Jimmy, "and a fort and a new football and a knife and one of them big selection boxes and that book of aeroplanes like Derek Bradshaw has and..." Shurrup! I said. I didn't even get to ask, did ya see? Did ya see what that Elf did? She bundled me out and now he's buggered off for his bloomin' dinner.

"Whoa," said Jimmy, "'appen you'll have to write to him then." And I was just about to thump him when me Dad came round the aisle corner.

"Right, lads," he said, "Ready for some grub?" And Jimmy ran up to him, rattling off that damn list again. Me Dad smiled at first but it seemed to fade as Jimmy got past the football.

"And what did you ask for son?" he said to me. I never got chance, I said, that bloomin' Elf pulled me out and he's gone for his dinner. It wasn't bloomin' fair!

"Dinner? Champion idea," said me Dad, "Let's us go and have some anorl." And we all marched out and met me mother on the pavement outside.

"Mucky Duck then, mother?" said Dad, lickin his lips and lookin down the street towards the traffic corner.

"You're not taking these lads to the pub for their dinner!" said Mam, the way she says things when you know she isn't going to say 'em again cos she doesn't have to. "Betty's," she said, "we'll go to Betty's for a nice sandwich and a cup o'tea." But I could tell me Dad was wanting more than a cup o'tea to put him right. See, me Dad didn't like Christmas shopping, he didn't like any shopping. In fact he bloody hated it cos I heard him tell me Grandad every week.

"Aw, come on love, they do a lovely sandwich in t'Mucky Duck, and you can have a small sherry."

"I do not *need* a small sherry, thank you very much!" said Mam, and she turned, grabbin our Jimmy's sleeve. "You go where you like," she said, "and you make up your mind anorl," she said to me, "sharpish!"

"Comin' wi' me, son?" said Dad, smiling now cos he'd got his way and you could tell he was already tasting the beer.

Half a minute later me and him were in the Mucky Duck, although some people call it the White Swan, like the sign over the door says. It was real busy, but me Dad soon caught Poker's eye. Poker worked behind the bar, and, funnily enough, he only had one eye to catch. He'd had the other one poked out in a fight years ago, so they say, during Scottish fortnight.

He also had a funny hand with some fingers missing. Dad said he used to work on a farm and lost 'em in a grass reaper and they used to call him Thumber, cos that's all he had left on his right hand.

They said he was daft for losing his fingers but when he came to work at the pub and lost his eye trying to stop a fight they said he was very brave, which I know means the same as clever. At some point they stopped calling him Thumber and started calling him Poker. I suppose he must have a real name somewhere, but nobody seems to know what it is.

"Pint please, Poker, and a still orange for the lad, oh and a couple o'growlers, please, ta." Great, I thought, we're having a growler for dinner. Mam and some other mothers called 'em pork pies but they're growlers really.

"Here, go and sit over there at that table, I'll bring yer grub in a minute." So I carried me orange across and sat near the fire. There was another man using the table as well but there was an empty chair so I climbed on, being careful not to spill me drink.

"Ey up, young 'un," said the old man, looking up from his sandwich. Hello, I said.

"Derek! What sauce do you want with yer growler?" called me Dad from over at the bar, and everybody could hear him. See, I always have tomato sauce, on everything, especially on chips and sausages, and always on growlers, but me Dad always has HP and he'd been trying to get me to have some. Says tomato's for girls. Says I'll never be a man if I don't have HP, but it doesn't half burn yer tongue. Anyway, I thought, I'm in a pub and folks are looking so it's probably best if I say HP.

HP, Dad! I said, as if I always had HP. I thought about asking for hot mustard anorl, but then me Dad would have taken the mickey in front of everybody and I'd be worse off than if I'd said tomato sauce, so I didn't.

I was starving for me growler, so when Dad put the plate down in front o'me I was right in. I dipped the edge of pie crust in the brown sauce and had a bite. Ooh!

"Burns a bit, eh lad?" said the old bloke next to me. Aye, I said.

"Here," he said, "have some tomato on it. Nowt like tomato sauce on a bit o'pie," and he pushed his bottle across to me. Thank-you, I said. And I looked at him properly for the first time, like Mam said you should when you say thank-you to somebody. And I saw his glasses. Round. Black. Mended in the middle with Sellotape.

"Looking forward to Christmas are you?" he said. Yeah, I think so. "Aye, thought you would be. How old are ya?" Nearly ten. "Oh, you won't be bothered about Father Christmas then, all them toys and stuff, nowt in your line I don't suppose." I knew he was teasing me, but you can't always tell when it's a stranger. I just filled me mouth wi' growler and took a big drink of orange so I didn't have to talk back. I'd seen me Dad do that at home when Mam was nagging him.

"Aye, Christmas," said the old man, and he turned to look into the fire. "Not what it was," he said. I looked across at Dad, to see if he was watching me or getting ready to leave but he was getting another pint and talking to Poker about the horseracing on t'telly.

"No. Not what it was. Kids not what they were. No. Songs, though. The songs. Some o'the old songs... Nice." I wasn't sure if he was talking to me now or to himself, like me Grandad does.

He took a big drink of his pint and wiped his mouth on his sleeve. Then he coughed and spat in the fire, where it sizzled for a minute. Then he looked at me and smiled.

"*Away in a manger, no crib for a bed...*" he was singing. At me. "*The little Lord Jesus lay down his sweet head.*"

Nobody much was listening, but it was right in me face so I couldn't help but hear.

"*The stars in the bright sky looked down where he lay, the little Lord Jesus asleep on the hay.*"

People had stopped talking now and most of 'em were staring at us. I looked down at me plate and was wishin' that I hadn't finished me growler and drunk me orange so quick, cos now I had nothing to do. Nothing to even look at. I should have gone to Betty's with Mam.

"*The cattle are lowing the baby awakes, but little Lord Jesus... no crying he... makes.*" He kept stoppin' and something in me throat was starting to burn, maybe the brown sauce.

"*I love thee Lord Jesus... look... down from...*" He was struggling... his eyes seemed to get all wet... "*the... sky.*" Then silence.

It was taking ages, so I couldn't help but finish it. *And stay by my side until morning is nigh.* It was real quiet now. They'd even turned the telly off. I didn't know where to look and me face got real hot.

Then the old man reached across and put his hand over the top of mine, and he coughed again and spat in the fire, and while it was sizzling people started talking again. They put the telly back on. He sniffed.

"So, tell me, what is it you're wanting for Christmas, young man?" A bow, I said, a bow and arrow.

"Away Derek lad, let's be back to meet yer mother," me Dad was calling across from the bar.

"A bow?" said the old man. "A real one I reckon, with proper arrows."

Yes, I said, a real one, not rubber, not a small one, not pretend, not... and me Dad collared me and pulled me away towards the door.

"Aye," said the old man, "a bow. I thought as much."

I never saw that old man ever again. In that pub or anywhere else. Never. But funny thing was... I got a bow and arrow that Christmas. A real one.

9

Strange Holly

We were at me Aunt Judy's house. We'd come on t'bus to bring her some presents and so me Mam could help her get ready for Christmas.

It took ages to get there, and we had to walk the last mile from the bus stop to the cottage and it rained. But I like me Aunt Judy. I used to like me uncle Tommy anorl, but he died last Easter. Heart attack. I know they're bad, them, heart attacks. And I know it's kids that give 'em to people, cos me Mam always says, when she catches me or our Jimmy doing owt daft, like hanging out of the bedroom widow, or if we hide behind the settee then jump up and give her a scare, wi' tomato sauce on our faces like pretend blood, she'll say "Ee, you daft little beggars you'll give me a heart attack!"

But Aunt Judy and Uncle Tommy didn't have any kids, so I don't know who gave him one. Any road, it killed him.

This was Aunt Judy's first Christmas on her own, and Mam said it was going to be sad for her. So that's why we'd all trailed through 'ere, to bring a few early presents and help her get ready. Though she was probably going to come back to our house and spend Christmas with us, according to Mam.

Me Dad said they were better off for not having kids, but me Aunt Judy always seemed like she'd be good at being somebody's mother. I would have had her. Sometimes.

Mam said Aunt Judy didn't feel much like getting ready for Christmas, and after all the grief I heard Mam giving Dad this morning I though aye, and she isn't the only one.

Why do mams say they love Christmas when they always hate getting ready for it? Maybe it's a bit like having the Sunday night bath. You hate getting ready for that, having to get undressed and being all cold, but it's nice when you finally get in. Specially if it's your turn to be first.

Anyway, we made Aunt Judy a cup o'tea then Mam told us all what we had to do. She'd start the Christmas baking while Dad and Jimmy did the decorations. I had to take the rubbish out, then get the coal in and stack some logs and kindling next to t'kitchen range, enough to last all Christmas week. Our Jimmy had cold so Mam said he couldn't go out.

Well, I soon had my jobs done so then I thought I'd show Jimmy how to go on with the streamers, cos he was bloomin' useless, but he wasn't having it. Neither was me Dad. Or me Mam.

Best thing about being in somebody else's house is that when your Mam and Dad get vexed with you they can't shout and swear like they do at home, or belt you one. They have to pretend to be nice. Mind, you know you'll get it when you get home.

Me Aunt Judy had just finished her cup o'tea and said, "It's alright, me and Derek'll get out of your way. It's faired up now so we'll go for a nice walk and get some holly, won't we love?" So much for me doing the streamers then.

"Are you sure?" said Mam, "Wouldn't you rather sit by the fire, love, and rest a minute, have a bit o'peace and quiet?" That's a laugh, I thought, peace and quiet in 'ere, with me Dad about to strangle our Jimmy wi't'Christmas lights cos he won't stop moaning and wiping his nose on the chair arm.

"Oh yes," said Aunt Judy, "we'll be grand, won't we, Derek? We could do with some fresh air." She maybe could, but I'd had me fill o'fresh air and fresh rain while I was walking all t'way from that bloomin' bus stop. But I didn't turn awkward, I just put me wellies back on and buttoned me coat up. And she put her coat on, and some zip-up boots with furry tops.

Just as we opened the back door, Mam stopped sifting her flour and looked at me. "Right, you behave yourself, me lad," then she said, "Do you think you could find me some holly, and a nice bit of ivy while you're out?"

See, Mam had been learning about fancy table decorations at the Women's Institute, and she'd an idea to make summat out of an old log and some fir cones and ivy. She'd got the fir cones out of the cemetery last week, on the sly, but was still wanting some ivy.

"Oh, I'm sure we can find that," said Aunt Judy, and we got set off, up the backyard and across the back field then along the bridle path. Aunt Judy wasn't saying much. Mam said not to mention about Uncle Tommy, so I didn't. We just walked. And walked, for ages.

I liked it round here, it was a lot different to round by us. Bigger trees. Bigger hedges. More chance of seeing a fox, or a pheasant, or a badger. And less chance of getting a good hiding off the kids from Peasey Hill.

Then suddenly there was one. A kid. He came out of a hole in the hedge and stood on the path right in front of us. Aunt Judy didn't say anything, just kept on walking, but he was right in front o'me so I had to stop.

He looked funny. Even more funny than Peasey Hill kids. Funny clothes, sort of homemade, a big red flat cap, and big boots... no socks.

He was about same age as me, maybe older, but a bit smaller, and apart from his red knees he was filthy.

"Ey up!" he said. Aye aye, I said, and I looked for Aunt Judy, but she was still walking away down the path, hadn't even noticed us.

"What's your name, then?" Er, it's Derek, I said. "Oh aye. Mine's Jackie." And somehow, I knew he wasn't going to hit me, or make any trouble. He was smiling. "Where y'off?" We're, er, we're off to get some holly, me and me Aunt Judy, for Christmas.

"Aye, I thought so." And he set off down the path in them great boots, so I followed. He slowed down a bit to let me come alongside, then we walked together, about five yards behind Aunt Judy. We weren't speaking but it was alright. He was whistling. Seemed quite capped with himself.

About ten minutes later we came to the end of the proper path and it widened out into a boggy gateway, leading onto a grass field. Aunt Judy stopped.

"Ooh, Derek," she said, "it's a bit plothery, can we get through?"

"Aye, course we can," said Jackie, and he took hold of her hand. I took hold of her other one and we tip-toed through the muck, minding the slap 'oles and being careful not to let her slip, or get her furry tops all plothered up.

When we got back onto some good going she looked down at me and said, "Thank-you, Derek, you're a proper little gentleman." But she never said owt to Jackie. She just raised the hand he'd been holding up to her cheek, and left it there for a bit, and looked over yonder, at nowt in particular. As if she'd forgotten summat. Like... gloves.

"C'mon, this way," said Jackie, and he set off along the edge of the field. I went after him, and Judy followed me.

"Derek, do you know where you're going?" Aye, appen, I said. We followed Jackie, along the hedgeback, round a bend, past a dead crow and then I could see it, just over there in the corner of the field, about fifty yards off, behind a barbed wire fence that was broken down. There was a pond. And right at the back was a tree. A holly tree. A champion holly tree.

"There y'are," said Jackie. "That holly tree's been there since God was a lad."

Aunt Judy hadn't seen it yet, cos she'd found an old tree stump in the hedgeback, all covered with ivy.

"Ooh look, Derek, some lovely ivy here for your Mam." And she started to pick at it, real dainty like, the way girls do. Me and Jackie left her to it and set off towards the pond, when she suddenly looked up and shouted, "Derek, don't go near that pond. It's not safe. D'you hear me?"

I stopped and turned round. It's alright, I said, we're just off to get some holly. But she was getting right upset over it.

"No, I mean it, you must keep away from that pond, it's not safe!" This was one of them times when she seemed just like a mother. But what about the holly? I said. "Never mind the holly, it's not worth it."

What's she mean not worth it? I thought, the bloody stuff's free. All I have to do is get round the side o'that pond and I'll be at it. Much as I want. Mind, the pond had steep sides and it was real greasy. Nowt to hang onto. Easy to slip.

"Derek, please listen to me, promise me you'll keep away. Promise. It's *dangerous!*"

Aye, well right there's the difference between women who are just women, and women who are mams. Cos women who are mams know damn well you never say it's *dangerous* to a kid, cos that's just like saying it's real good fun. You might as well say Go on, do it, I dare you, it'll be great. Aunt Judy wasn't a mam and so she didn't know about kids and dangerous, but I didn't want to upset her any more than she already was. And at least we were getting some ivy. Holly could wait. I could come back wi'Jimmy later.

Aye, alright, I said, I'll only go as far as t'fence, just to have a look, alright?

"Alright then, just to the fence but not a step further, and please be careful." I didn't like her being upset and all, and I certainly didn't want to give her an 'eart attack, but I did want a look at that pond. We don't have any ponds round by us in the village, apart from Mrs Hardwick's little concrete job in her posh front garden, full o'goldfish and a daft gnome with a fishing rod. And he's got an arm missing.

I walked up to the barbed wire fence, and then I noticed summat. Jackie was gone. I know he'd come across here while I was talking to Aunt Judy, and there was nowhere else to go. It was a dead end. He can't have just disappeared. But he had. I looked back towards Aunt Judy, and she was still picking at the ivy, bundling long strands up under her arm, and looking across at me every two seconds. Keeping a close eye on me. I gave her a thumbs up, Alright? She didn't smile.

I looked back at the pond, and saw some footprints in the mud, heading around the side, it was the only way you could get to the tree cos it was surrounded on every other side by barbed wire or brambles. Then I saw the footprints finish, right by a long scrape sort of a mark, where it looked like somebody had slipped, down the bank into the water.

Jackie? I said, Jackie? And then I saw his cap. Floating there, in the middle of the pond. No ripples or ought, just his red cap floating there, right in the middle. On all that dark green water. And as I watched, wondering what do to next, it sank. Clean out of sight. Gone. You couldn't tell it had ever been there.

Aunt Judy? I said. Aunt Judy! *Quick, I think Jackie's fallen in t'pond!* She ran across to me.

"What did you say?"

Jackie, that lad that came with us, he's gone! Must have tumbled in, slipped down that bank, into t'water! I just saw his red cap, floatin on t'top, over there in t'middle, then it just sank! He's tumbled in!

She stopped. Dead still. She dropped the ivy and grabbed both me hands, and closed her eyes. Some people can cry big tears even when their eyes are closed. Me Aunt Judy could.

Shouldn't we do summat? I said. Send for somebody, try and get him out? She breathed in, real deep, then she opened her eyes, they were a bit red.

"Derek," she said, "you're not to do this. You're not to say anything about Jackie Webster. Not another word. Please. Not a word! *Do you understand?*"

Well, I didn't really, but she was getting more upset by the minute, and how did she know his last name was Webster? He never told me and he never even spoke to her. Oh, I don't like it when women cry, whether or not they're mams. People who cry usually need a cuddle, and she was too big, I couldn't reach.

I looked back at the pond. It was dead calm. Not a ripple. Just flat and green. Dark green. It could have been six inches deep, or six miles, you'd never know. Jackie was in there. Least I think he was. Where else could he be?

She grabbed me hand and pulled me away, picked up the ivy again and we set off back along the hedgeside, down past the muddy gateway and up the path, back to the cottage. She was holding me hand real tight. We were walking quite fast, as if we had a bus to catch. She never said a word, all the way. Just a sniff now and then.

When we got through the gate, into her backyard she stopped and turned to me, and let go of me hand. Then she pulled me in close and gave me a big hug, and bent down to kiss me on the nose. Then she whispered in me ear.

"Derek, I'm sorry for getting upset, and I know you'll think I'm behaving very badly, but I got very afraid. I knew a boy called Jackie, many years ago. I wasn't much older than you are now. Jackie was in my class at school. He was my sweetheart." She pulled her hankie out and dabbed at her eyes. "He... he wore a bright red cap, lovely it was. But one day, just before Christmas, he went off by himself to gather some holly from that tree by the pond, and he..." she started crying again, "no one ever saw..."

Then me Dad opened the back door, "Ey up, you're back then! You must have heard t'kettle boiling, and there's some corned beef sandwiches just made. Ey, but mind them that's pressed well down at t'edges. Jimmy made them."

Aunt Judy gave me all the ivy to hold while she gave her face a proper wipe with the hankie, saying summat to Dad about how warm she'd got walking back so quickly.

"Some right ivy you got there, son," said me Dad, "but no holly, then?" Me and Aunt Judy looked at each other but we didn't say anything. He laughed. "Never mind, let's away in and show your mother. She'll be right capped."

We went inside and Aunt Judy was still all hankies and wiping so nobody could see she'd been crying. It was nice and warm, and smelled of fresh baking. Mam was covered in flour but she poured us all a cup o'tea and thanked Aunt Judy for the ivy. She promised to make her one of whatever it was the Women's Institute said you could make with some ivy and pine cones and an old log.

Dad passed round the plate of sandwiches. Aunt Judy looked for one with pressed down edges and thanked Jimmy very much for making it. "It's so the meat doesn't fall out," he said. And it didn't.

Aunt Judy's cottage looked real nice. Dad had done a champion job o'the decorations, a little tree set up near the window with our presents underneath, and even the lights were working. Well, most of 'em. There were cards on the mantle piece, and candles ready to light, and streamers going from corner to corner. And twigs of holly with bright red berries on top of all the picture frames. Ey up a minute. Holly?

Ey Dad, I said, Where d'you get that holly?

"Ha!" said me Dad, "Funny you should you ask that. Daftest thing. We were all through here in t'back kitchen when we heard a knock at t'front door." Mam and Jimmy were nodding.

"I went straight away but when I opened it whoever it was had gone, no sign, just disappeared... but there on t'front door step was a lovely bundle of holly, fresh picked, and whoever brought it left some muddy footmarks. Right plothery mess, but don't worry Judy love, I rinsed mud off with a bucket o'water. Any road, we brought it in and there you are. Were you expecting some, Judy?"

I looked at me Aunt Judy, but she was buried in hankies again.

"Well mother," said me Dad, "We'd best be setting off for that bus in a minute, unless we're walking all t'way back."

"Right you are," said Mam, "and are you going to come to us for Christmas then?" she said, to Aunt Judy. Everybody went quiet. I'm not sure who wanted Aunt Judy to come to our house and who didn't. I think we all did. Mind, she'd have to sleep on t'settee so I don't know how that would sit with Father Christmas.

"No, love," said Aunt Judy, "Thank you very much, very kind, but I'm alright here. I'll have a nice Christmas now, very cosy, thanks to you."

Mam looked a bit upset. And Jimmy. It would have been nice to have Aunt Jusy with us for Christmas.

"Yes, I'm all set," she said, "You've got me coal in, and some logs, and me baking's all done, and I have all these wonderful decorations. And best of all, I have me holly. Me beautiful holly..."

We put our coats and wellies on and got ready for off. Aunt Judy went round us all saying goodbye and Merry Christmas, and everybody got a kiss and a hug. Mam made sure to wipe Jimmy's nose before it was his turn. I got an extra long hug, and a wink.

"I mean, what is Christmas after all," she said, "but memories? And if we're not making memories together, we're enjoying them."

"Bit like Christmas baking, eh!" said Dad, and he pulled a mince pie out of his coat pocket and shoved the whole thing into his mouth. Crafty beggar.

10

Crafty

Me Mam had known about it for ages. That's why she'd spent all this time knitting and making pots o'jam and chutney and all that. But she only told us lot tonight, while we were busy watching a cowboy on t'telly.

"Don't forget we've got the craft fair, this coming Saturday," she said, just as me Dad was shooting a baddy off a clifftop. "Eh?" said Dad, and slowly blew the smoke from his finger end, twirled it round and put it down the top of his trousers, and had a quick scratch while he was in there.

"Beggin' your pardon, ma'am?" he said, sounding just like Roy Rogers, if Roy Rogers had come from Pickering.

"The half and half craft fair, at the village hall, I told you last month."

"You told me nowt."

"I did anorl but you're either deaf or daft."

"Or both," said our Jimmy.

"The village hall is having a Christmas craft fair to raise funds, where folks can sell any Christmassy stuff they've made and keep half the profits."

"Oh aye, and what happens to t'other half?" said Dad.

"The village hall keeps it, cos it's a fundraiser, to raise funds, you great daft 'apeth," Mam said, and I thought she did well not to belt him one cos even I could work out where the brass was going.

"So, I've got my knitting all ready, some socks, mittens, baby's bootees, a scarf or two... oh yes, and a nice balaclava helmet." Thank god she's selling that, I thought, it'll save me having to look daft in it. And they itch like a bugger do them bacalavas.

"And I'm making some apple chutney and damson jam."

"Ey, I like that damson jam!" said Dad.

"Good, you can buy some then," she said. "So, what are you lot making to sell?"

I thought for minute. This was chance to make some money, and I just happened to need some. Come to think of it, I always need some money, cos I never have any.

"We've been making Christmas stuff at school, Mam," said our Jimmy, and for once he was right. Aye, I said, they're making some pretend candles out of the middle of toilet rolls, and we've been bending a few pipe cleaners to look like skinny reindeer.

"So that's where all the bloomin' toilet roll middles have been going." See! I told you she'd notice! I said to him.

He'd gone into the cupboard under the bathroom sink last week and been taking the toilet roll middles out by squashing 'em then poking a wooden spoon through the hole to push the cardboard out. Then, when you put the rolls on the holder in the toilet they weren't round anymore so they didn't roll. They just went *wump wump wump* when you pulled the paper off. I knew somebody'd notice.

Me Dad'd been thinking all this time, probably about money like the rest of us, then he piped up. "Right then, I'll make some stuff to sell anorl. Every day this week during me dinner break I'll make summat in t'factory workshop. Old Charlie Nendick'll see me right for some bits o'wood and stuff."

"Don't you be getting sacked just before Christmas," Mam said. She didn't hold with stealing, and she was the only one in our house who didn't do it, which made it a lot easier when stuff went missing. Cos whenever I had owt nicked I knew it was either me Dad or our Jimmy. And it was never me Dad.

"No, it'll be right, and I'll tell 'em it's for a very good cause," he winked at me.

Next day was Monday and after tea we all showed each other what we'd made. Jimmy had three of them toilet roll candles, painted red. Well mostly red. I think he'd run out o'red and finished 'em wi' brown, and you could see the bits he'd missed where he'd been holding 'em with his other hand. I had four pipe cleaner reindeers - two white, one green and one grey, cos that's all I could grab while the teacher wasn't looking.

Mam opened a cupboard door and there was a row of little jars. Damson jam, and we could have guessed that cos the house smelled of it, and we'd had the scrapings from round the pan on some bread for our tea.

Then it was Dad's turn. He stood up and put a carrier bag on the table, then he rolled up his sleeves and, like a magician taking a rabbit out of a top hat, he reached in and slowly pulled out summat made o'wood. A bit like a box but with a triangle bit on the top. Then he turned it round and showed us a little hole in one side.

"Bird house!" he said, real capped with himself.

"And what sort o'bird could possibly squeeze itself into that?" asked Mam.

"A real skinny 'un," said Jimmy.

"Well it was t'biggest drill bit I could find," said Dad. "Any road, it'll do for Jenny Wren."

That's what you should call it, Dad, I said. *Wren's Den*, and I went to get a wax crayon to write it on for him.

Every day that week we kept making stuff, and telling each other it was good, even when it was rubbish. We kept it all in a big cardboard box in the front passage. We were going to make loads o'money at this here fair.

On Friday night, Dad couldn't wait until after tea and he pulled his daily creation out of the carrier as soon as he came in.

"Now then, 'ere's champion... look ya there!"

Well. We looked. It was a... a scrubbing brush nailed onto a piece o'board, with two buttons stuck on the front, like eyes, and a rusty bent nail for a nose. It looked like a cross-eyed hedgehog that had been run over.

"Hedgehog shoe scraper," he said, "Well, hedgehog shoe brusher, for brushing the muck off your boots, at t'back door."

"Looks like it's been run over," said Jimmy.

"Aye, well, that was t'only brush I had... it wanted a bigger, fatter one really, but any road."

Mam had been watching, but turned back to look out the kitchen window. And I don't know why, cos it was pitch black outside and you couldn't see much. But maybe it had just dawned on her where her new scrubbing brush had gone from under the sink. The one she asked me about this morning, after me Dad had gone to work.

So, Saturday morning finally rolls round and we had to put our good clothes on and then walk over to the village hall carrying all our crafts. Mam had a nice shopping basket with all her jams and knitted stuff, but the rest of us just had a load o'carrier bags.

Jimmy was late getting ready and couldn't find his good shoes, but Mam said we were leaving him so he had to run to catch us up. He'd found the shoes but not the time to tie 'em, so just as he reached us he tripped up on his laces and went flying. He landed on his carrier bag so it was alright and he didn't bleed.

When we got there Mrs Dicker showed us which was our table, right down in t'far corner where it was a bit dark, and we got set up. Jimmy's candles looked a bit squashed where he'd fallen on 'em, but I told him they were alright, well, for a penny apiece, anyway. I was asking twopence each for me reindeer but Dad was struggling to think of a price for his birdhouse and hedgehog scraper thing.

"Bloomin' brush alone cost me one and six," said Mam, so he asked for two shillings. *Wren's Den* was "attractively priced", according to Dad, at half a crown.

Some women came over and bought some jam off Mam and a pair of socks she'd knitted. I was hoping she'd sell the bacalava early on else there was a damn good chance I'd be getting it for Christmas. Nobody bought owt off me or me Dad, or Jimmy, so we went for a walk round, see what else there was.

There was a woman selling biscuits and homemade fudge, and she had a load of little pieces on a plate at the front of her table, so you could try 'em. Me and Jimmy got a good handful each, to make summat like a mouthful, but we didn't have any money to buy owt, so we just thanked her and left her to cut up some more bits.

The fudge made our mouths all claggy so me Dad bought us a glass of dandelion and burdock each from a big table of food and drink they'd set up near the kitchen. I like dandelion and burdock. It tastes funny, and I've no idea how many dandelions they put in, and I don't even know what burdock is, but I like it. I think there's a lot more to it than lemonade.

"Ey, Jim," Dad said, "best fasten that shoelace up me lad, before you up-end yersen again." But he didn't.

Right next to the door where everybody came in was Simon Cartwright and his little sister Mary. Right snobby little devils they are. Live in a big posh house at the top of the street. Both in the church choir but he's crap at football. They had a load of angels they'd made, going for threepence each. And they were selling fast anorl.

Simon said he'd made the bodies out of clothespegs then she'd stuck on some bits of white white material for a dress and painted smiley faces on 'em. Right sissy looking stuff it was. All sparkling clean, like them kids that go to Sunday school. Well, they were clean until Jimmy tripped over his lace again and slopped his dandelion and burdock all over their table.

We ran for it before Simon Cartwright even knew what happened. When we snuck by a few minutes later they didn't look much like angels anymore. More like zombies coming out of a swamp.

There was a table full of knitted poodles that some old women had made, and they had toilet rolls inside. I saw our Jimmy's eyes light up but I told him to keep his thieving mits off else we'd get slung out. Me Dad came over and picked one up for a look. There were some wooden toilet brushes that had been made to look like sunflowers with some orange petals stuck on the handle.

"Aye, but it's still just a toilet brush," said Dad, "and any road, I don't like toilet brushes, I much prefer paper!" And he laughed real loud and the old women gave him the kind o'look they usually give dogs that have just done their business on the footpath.

That dandelion and burdock had gone straight through me so I had to go to the toilet. When I went in I heard somebody in one of the cubicles, having a number two. They were pulling toilet paper off, *wump wump wump*. Ey up, I thought, our Jimmy's been in there for some craft supplies.

I finally got back to our table and it was just about empty. All except for the bacalava. Ey Mam, I said, Where's all our stuff? She just smiled at me.

"She reckons it's all been sold," said Dad, who was scratching his head, which makes a change from what he usually scratches, and he was pulling the tablecloth up to look underneath, in case the stuff had all fallen down there.

"All of it, Mam?" said Jimmy, "Every candle?"

"Every last one, love," she said. "We've sold out! And here's your money." She dug into her apron pocket and gave me a shilling, and Jimmy got ten pence.

"What about my stuff, love?" said Dad.

"Gone," she said, "Surprisingly enough, it's actually gone. There's no accounting for taste." And she gave him a fair

handful of coins out of her apron. I thought to meself it's alright is this craft fair lark. I 'ope we do it again next year. I could make hundreds of them reindeer before next Christmas.

A few days later, I was rooting through the cupboard under the sink, looking for some Domestos to get rid of a mark I'd made on the kitchen floor with some white paint. I'd been trying to do some snowflakes on the windows, as a surprise for Mam and Dad, but I'd spilt. Anyway, I came across a scrubbing brush. It looked a bit like the new one Mam lost, but there was a few holes in it, like nail holes. I'm sure it was Dad's hedgehog shoe scraper thing, I'm positive. But I never said ought.

Then on Christmas eve, when Dad lifted me and Jimmy up to touch the angel on top of the Christmas tree before we went to bed, like we always do for good luck, I saw three pipe cleaner reindeer clinging on to some of the branches at the back. Mam must have pinched my idea and made some herself. I looked at her, but she was busy reading.

I didn't see any pretend candles, though. And by gum was I relieved when Christmas morning finally came and we opened all the presents and I didn't get that stupid bacalava. Aye, but I bet some poor sod did.

11

Church

Me Mam was opening the Christmas cards that came in the post this morning. And she was tutting. The way she does when she doesn't like summat.

"*Tut*. Why does she always do that?" Nobody was listening. We could all hear her but nobody was listening. "*Tut*. Ee, it does get on me nerves, it does really."

We all knew that somebody had to say summat, to ask her what it was that got on her nerves. We all knew that we did, but this was summat else. Me Dad was first to volunteer. He looked at me and Jimmy, then put down his paper.

"What gets on your nerves, love?"

"Xmas," she said.

"Eh?" said Dad, "I thought you *liked* Christmas."

She does like it anorl, so I thought she was just getting strained again from all the fettling and shopping and stuff she does to get ready, and I didn't reckon it was ought much to think about. But then she said "Course I do, I love *Christmas*, but I don't like *Xmas* one little bit!"

Me Dad looked at me and Jimmy again and pulled one of his faces and shook his head a bit, just a little bit, but enough for Mam to catch him.

"I mean," she said, throwing a screwed-up envelope and getting him right on the nose-end, "people who write Xmas instead of Christmas, that's what I can't stand. It's just bloomin' lazy, that's all it is. They can't be bothered to write Christ so they put an X instead."

"Maybe he doesn't want any publicity if he wins the pools," said Dad and laughed real loud. Mam just tutted again. He can be real daft can me Dad, and he knows it gets on Mam's nerves.

"People seem to forget what Christmas is all about."

She was talking to all of us now, or else nobody at all. It sounds the same either way.

"We're supposed to be celebrating the birth of Jesus Christ, but most folks think it's just an excuse to eat and drink too much."

89

That's a rum 'un, I thought, cos at least ten times a day she'd say to me and our Jimmy, "I don't want an argument!" and here she was asking for one. Dad kept quiet, but she didn't.

"I mean, you've just got to look at the shops haven't you? It's all buy this and get that and hang these up... and never a mention of the nativity."

"You just mentioned it," said Dad, who was really pushing his luck now. Mam stood up and put the card on the mantelpiece, among the others we'd got. Then she bent down and put a bit more coal on t'fire.

"You know," she said, "we'd always go to church on Christmas Eve, every single year, ever since I can remember... 'til I got married." She looked at me Dad. "When I was little, me grandad used to carry me through the snow on his shoulders and bend down to get under the church door, I remember that." She was definitely in a talking to everybody but nobody mood now.

"It was always full, and there'd be candles all along the walls, and evergreens across the altar. Ee, and the organ and the carols were beautiful." She was looking through the wall now, like she often does, as though there was a window there with a nice view. But there isn't.

"Then, after the singing and the lessons, they'd throw open both the big wooden doors and we'd come out of church after midnight, so it was Christmas Day." Bloomin' 'eck, I thought, that must have been a long service. Mam was still thinking back and looking through the wall.

"We'd all wish each other *Merry Christmas!* Shaking hands and hugging, kissing, ha!... And we'd walk home singing the carols again, all the way." She stopped talking but kept gawpin'.

"We went one year," said me Dad, "to church, aye, we did anorl!"

"One year?" said Mam, as if she'd just been woken up.

"Aye, we went to church, we did. It was the year me Dad got lost on the way back from t'pub, thick fog, real pea-souper, so we all went out to look for him."

"Did you round up a posse to go and get him like cowboys do on telly, Dad?" said Jimmy.

"Aye, lad, we did," said Dad, "We were in a posse, but walking. Any road, seemed he'd been feeling his way along the church railings when he bumped into me great aunt Ena, just arriving for the Christmas Eve service. And when we finally got there she'd dragged us all in with her."

The whole posse? I said. "Aye lad, and it was that cold it was even foggy in church."

"Are you sure?" said Mam.

"It's right," he said, "Aye, it was old aunt Ena that dragged us in. Ey, you be careful lads, they'll do that to you will great aunties," he said, winking at me and Jimmy.

"Typical!" said Mam, "That's just typical of you." And she sniffed and straightened her pinny, like when somebody was in trouble. Ey up, I thought, we're going to get it now.

"Right!" she said, "This year we're all going to church."

"Eh?" said Dad, "You what you say?"

"This family, all of us, every one of us," she said, "We're all going to church on Christmas Eve to celebrate the birth of Jesus Christ."

"Do we have to buy him a present?" said Jimmy, but nobody heard. It went all quiet. Then Dad leaned over and let off. *Rarrt!*

"*Freddy!*" he shouted. He does that. Ever since we were little, Dad used to blame his farts on Freddy, an angry duck that lives in his underpants. He's real daft sometimes is our Dad. Anyway, me Mam usually gets mad when he does that, but all she could think about now was church.

"Yes, we're all going to church on Christmas Eve. That's final. Me mind's made up."

"Is me Grandad going to carry you on his shoulders, then?" said Jimmy. Nobody heard. Dad was gobsmacked, but me and Jimmy just looked at each other and laughed. We'd get to stay up late, and it might be a bit o'fun.

"And we're going to go smart. You'll be putting your best clothes on," she said.

Oh, so it wouldn't be much fun then. My best clothes were bloomin' awful. I had a best white shirt with a real stiff collar that dug into me neck, and a pair of scratchy best short trousers that didn't half itch. And I had a stupid best woolly cardigan that Mam knit me years ago, but it was growing as fast as I was, so I had to keep wearing it. It had great big wooden buttons, a real beggar to fasten. They were too big for the buttonholes, so she'd struggle and do 'em up before I left the house and I could never get 'em undone on me own. I had to wait until I got home. I sometimes spent all day fastened up in that bloomin' thing.

Mind, Jimmy was worse. He'd got a daft-looking sailor boy suit from our Granny last year that he had to wear when we went anywhere posh. All stripes and collars and little anchors stuck all over t'spot. He looked a right tater in that. He said he'd lost the stupid white hat that went with it, but I know for a fact the little sod threw it into t'river off Ryton Bridge when we were out on a walk, last bank holiday.

Christmas Eve was the night after next, so Dad hadn't got much time to get us out of this church thing. He wasn't at all keen, though, so I knew he'd try. And he did.

He was at work all day then when he came home, a bit earlier than usual, he had stories about being real busy on Christmas Eve. About having to go and help a mate put up a Christmas tree, then collect some sprouts from another bloke's allotment.

"Aye," said Mam, "that's as maybe, but you'll have that tree up in half an hour and we already have sprouts, so you'll be back here in plenty of time to give me a hand with a few jobs and get washed, shaved, and changed before ten o'clock, won't you?" It was one of them questions that Mam's good at. The kind that only have one answer and it never needs saying, so he didn't.

Hey, staying up til past ten o'clock was going to be alright. We wouldn't get to bed until, ooh, after midnight. Sean Collins at school always stays up while midnight on Christmas Eve at their house, and then they get to open one present each, before bed. Mind, I think they're Catholics so the presents might not be up to much.

Just for a laugh, I got the bible down from the shelf in the front room, and had a flick through. Aye, well, it wasn't much of a laugh, some daft looking words in there, and a lot of 'em in that slopey printing, but I did find the bit about the baby Jesus being born in a manger in Bethlehem. They went on a lot about other stuff and it was ages before I got to the shepherds and I never did find the wise men. Maybe they'd liven it up a bit at church, though Vicar Dicker wasn't much good at telling stories.

Anyway, Christmas Eve finally came, and Dad got home from work in good time and said the bloke he was supposed to help had already done his tree, so he didn't have to go anywhere. He seemed a bit sad about it. We had our teas, which was a bit of a plain do, cos Mam said we'd be eating a lot of rich food and goodies over Christmas, so we only had beans on toast, as usual.

It got to about eight o'clock and Mam said she'd like me Granny and Grandad to come anorl, so she sent me round to their house to tell 'em.

"Say we'll be calling by at about half-past ten, and we can all walk up the street together."

I had to go on me own cos Jimmy had lost his wellies again. I thought about going to the shop as I went past, to get some Fruit Gums, but they were shut. I got to me Grandad's house and knocked on t'door, then I opened it and walked in, like I usually do. I got a bit of a shock. He was standing there in t'passage way, with his coat on.

"Ey up, Derek lad," he said, "what are you after? You aren't looking for Father Christmas are you cos he hasn't been here yet," and he laughed and tapped his walking stick on the floor, the way he does.

No, I said, me Mam said we're all off to Church tonight for midnight mast and I have to tell you and Gran to be ready by half-past ten and we'll call for you on the way up t'street. I wondered if I should say please somewhere among all this, but Mam wouldn't have, so I didn't.

"*Church?*" said Grandad, as if I'd asked him to meet us on t'moon wearing just his underpants. "*Church? Tonight?*"

Aye, Mam said we all have to go, last thing. Dad's not suited but we have to go. No arguing. And it's real late. Past bedtime really.

"Ee, Derek me lad, ah don't know about that." He sucked a lot of air past his false teeth, like a backwards whistle. "See, we're, er... well, er, 'appen we're watching telly tonight. Bing Crosby's on, aye that's it, *White Christmas.*"

Then me Granny came into the passage and she had her topcoat on anorl, and her hat and gloves. Must be real cold in their house tonight, I thought. Maybe they've run out o'coal. Grandad turned to speak to her.

"Young Derek says we have to go to church tonight. To church. *Tonight! Church!*"

She must have gone deaf, I thought, but she hadn't. She'd heard him alright, and then it was her turn to look as though she'd been asked to go to t'moon in just her knickers. I'd had enough. Alright then, I said, I'll tell me Mam. Bye Gran, see you in t'mornin'. Or else at church. Do you think it's going to snow, Grandad?

"Aye, well, stranger things have 'appened, lad," he said as I closed the door behind me and left 'em both standing in the passage, in the dark.

Course, Mam weren't well suited when I got back and told her. She started chuntering.

"Watching Bing Crosby instead o'going to church on Christmas Eve with his family? Watching *telly* instead of singing carols?" Me Dad kept quiet. He can be real good at that sometimes. Much better than me and Jimmy.

"Well, we'll just see about that," she said, and she tutted real loud then went back into the kitchen with her big scissors.

"What's it like at church, Dad?" said our Jimmy.

"Well son," Me Dad said, "you have a lot o'fun at church. That's what they do there, dole out fun to them as needs it. In fact, the more miserable you are, the more often you get to go."

Is that why we never go? I said.

"Aye, that's right, lad, we 'ave so much fun of our own we don't need none o'theirs." But what about me Mam? I said, Why's she so keen on going?

"Well," said Dad, "sometimes your Mam doesn't realise how much fun she's having here with us, so maybe she has to go to church every now and then just to remind herself," and he started reading the *Radio Times* as if that would shut us up. And it did.

Christmas Eve always goes so slowly, waiting for Father Christmas and all the presents. But this year it was going even slower, waiting for church. There was nowt on telly and Mam wouldn't let us have any Christmas baking, but made us some more toast instead. Dad was having one last go at the Christmas lights, and it sounded like he was getting all his bad words out of the way before church.

We all ended up in the bathroom together, trying to get washed and ready, and I couldn't find me good shoes so I had to put me old ones on, and that made Mam a bit mad.

"We'll have to sit at the back now!" she said, "I can't take you anywhere, Derek!"

"'Appen he should wear his wellies anyway," said Dad, "cos they're talking about snow tonight." But Mam wasn't having any wellies in church, so we all got our coats on and set off.

"Do you have change for the collection?" she asked Dad as we were walking up the street. I saw him put both hands in his pockets, but he never said anything.

Walking past the pub me Mam glanced through the front window, and she suddenly stopped dead. There, leaning up against the bar and raising his beer glass higher than everyone else, was me Grandad. Gran was sat on a bench near the fire, with a big glass of sherry and some tinsel on her hat.

"*Right!* Just you wait here!" said Mam, so we did, and she stormed into the pub. Half a minute later, Gran and Grandad were outside with us, chuntering a bit and struggling to get into their coats.

"I thought you two were watching Bing Crosby tonight," said Dad.

"Aye, we might be," said Grandad, "but he hasn't come in yet. He must be drinking in Malton."

And so we went to church, with Mam herding us along the footpath like a sheepdog, nipping at Grandad's heels now and then to keep him going. Granny wasn't well suited, and neither would the landlord be when he found out she'd nicked her sherry glass from the pub. She finished it off just as we got into the churchyard and stood the empty glass on a gravestone.

Mam didn't see, but Mr and Mrs Smith walking behind us did. Mr and Mrs Smith, he was called Fred, were what Mam called church regulars. Every week. Always dressed up posh. He usually took the collection plate round, she said, and was well in with Vicar Dicker.

Church was just about packed when we got inside, but we found a pew right at the back and Mam shuffled us all in. Dad first, then me and Jimmy, then Granny and Grandad, and Mam at the outside, to stop us escaping I suppose. Mr and Mrs Smith sat right in front of us.

Anyway, everybody quietens down and Vicar Dicker gets going and talks about how we're all gathered together to celebrate the birth of the blessed Christ Child, and he's hardly finished the first bit before our Jimmy's wriggling about and telling me he needs the toilet.

Mam's too far off for me to tell her and Granny's right next to him, but she's no good at stuff like this, and I think she's already nodding off. I elbowed me Dad and told him, but he just told me to shush and tell Mam. So I told Jimmy to shurrup and hold it in, whatever it was.

We stood up, just cos everybody else did, and sang the first hymn, *Away in a Manger*, and then Vicar Dicker said Mr Smith was going to read the lesson, so he got up and walked to the front. Huh! Some lesson. He just read two pages off the big bible they keep on the wooden ledge near where the choir sits.

Summat about the nativity and blessed children, but I didn't catch much cos Jimmy was still elbowing me and saying he was bustin'.

Mr Smith finished reading and came back to sit down, smilin' all the way. Vicar Dicker got back up and started talking about Mary's immaculate contraption and us all being blessed with Jesus' birth and what a holy, silent night it was in Bethlehem. And just as he finished saying that, when it was all real quiet, our Jimmy let off. *Raart!*

And it sounds real loud on them wooden pew things. It echoed right round the church, but quick as a flash Jim shouted "*Freddy!*" and everybody turned and stared at Mr Smith.

Well, I started laughing. So did Dad, but he managed to keep it a bit quieter. Granny sort of screamed and snorted and Grandad leaned over and started bangin' his stick on the floor, the way he does when he really likes summat. Jimmy was laughin' loudest and I thought well, whatever it is he's keepin' in won't stop there long.

Then Mam suddenly had us all stood up and leaving. She never said a word, she just sort of twitched her head and looked at us, like a sheepdog does with sheep who know they have to shift smartish if they don't want biting.

Course, the church business wasn't finished so everybody went quiet and just stared at us as we were walking away, and they hadn't opened the big doors for us. When we got outside it wasn't snowing, like I'd hoped. It was raining. Nobody had a brolly. Mam walked on in front of us, marching real quick, as if she'd left the oven on and was keen to get back.

I walked with me Dad while Jimmy got stuck between Granny and Grandad at the back, who were real slow and wondering aloud if the pub might still be open.

Dad was still laughing a bit, but he stopped when I said So, do blessed kids get more presents then, Dad?

"I don't know, son," he said, "but my blessed kids certainly aren't."

96

12

Pure Magic!

I remember. It was raining and we had to stay inside, even though I got a bike for Christmas. I think Father Christmas must have had a bit of a job on with it, cos some of the paint had been knocked off and the seat was a bit torn. But it was a nice bike.

I was busting to have a ride, but I just sat next to it in the hallway for a bit, polishing the handlebars, and ringing the bell, until me Mam threatened to belt me. I lifted the back end up and turned the pedal, watching the wheel spin round, then I got my finger caught in a spoke and said a loud swear word, which Mam just happened to hear.

So then I had to help make the dinner, peel a whole sinkful of spuds in cold water standing right next to her for an hour, and listening to some boring choir on the wireless singing hymns. Then a bloke called Ivory Manual came on and sang a song. Me and me Dad started singing along with him, but with the wrong words. Mam always says Christmas is a strain. Sometimes I can see what she means.

Mam had been up since six o'clock in the morning to do the big dinner, not long after me and our Jimmy got up. Jimmy got a meddy-evil fort for Christmas, not a bad 'un neither, real stone walls about a foot high made of plastic, but he didn't know how it all fixed together, and Mam didn't know cos she's useless at stuff like that. I couldn't help him cos it wasn't mine and I wasn't allowed to go near it. Grandad was no use cos he was still walking round from their house with Granny, but they had to go past the pub so me Dad said they weren't gonna be here for a long while.

Dad was still wrestling with the Christmas lights. We could hear him rattling, somewhere behind the tree. He'd been working on 'em for about two weeks now. Miss Gower, my teacher at school, would say he's very persistent. Mam just says he's bloody stubborn and always has been. I mean, everybody knows what it's like trying to get Christmas lights going. There's always one bulb that's not working. On our string there were 23 not working. In fact, only two lit up and one of them had all the paint chipped off it.

It was the same every bloomin' year. Me Dad would get the lights out of the attic two weeks before Christmas, and every year he seemed real surprised cos they weren't working. They never have worked. If you ask me, they get worse. I think we had five bulbs lit up last year.

Anyway, I read last year's *Beano* annual again then it was dinner time, so we sat in the kitchen, with the windows all steamed up, and waited for Granny and Grandad to come from the pub.

I'd set the table so I didn't think it was fair that Mam let Jimmy light the Christmas candle in the middle. So I opened the back door for a minute and the wind blew it out, then I lit it again.

We all got sick of waiting for the others so in the end me Dad had to go down and get 'em out of the pub, but they must have turned awkward in there cos it took him about twenty minutes.

When they did all get back it took 'em ages to get their coats off, then Granny put hers back on cos she says it's always cold in our house. And it bloomin' wasn't. Me Mam was red as a beetroot. So was Granny come to think of it. Any road, we finally all squashed in around the kitchen table and Mam stuck the big knife into the goose. It was a great dinner. I had three platefuls and Jimmy had two.

Then me Mam brought out the Christmas pudding, which me and Jimmy aren't too keen on, but there's usually a threepenny bit hidden inside so we always ask for a big lump. There was white sauce on it anorl, which looked brown because of the Lamb's Navy Rum me Mam likes to put in it. Me Dad tried to light it with a match, or more like half a box of matches, and burnt his finger. Him and Mam started arguing about which burns best, brandy or whisky. It didn't much matter cos we hadn't got either of 'em. I said we had some lighter fluid under the sink, but they just ignored me as usual.

In the end we had the pudding raw, without any flames, but it still seemed to taste alright. Granny had started sweatin so she took her coat off and had a big drink to cool down. Sherry it was.

As usual, though, it wasn't me that got the threepenny bit. This year it was Grandad. I wouldn't mind but he had a great pocketful already. He plays with coins. Me Grandad's a good magician, according to him. He can take a coin and make it disappear out of his hand, as long you're looking at the right hand, and then he makes it turn up in somebody's ear. He was sat between Granny and Mam, so he took the threepenny bit, made it disappear, looked at me and Jimmy as though he didn't know where it could have gone, then reached up behind Granny's left ear to dig for it.

"Bugger off George!" she said and elbowed him in the ribs. It knocked the wind out of him, and made him flip the threepenny bit halfway across the table, right into the jug of pudding sauce. It sat on the skin on the top, and for a minute I thought it was gonna float, but then it slipped beneath the surface, like a submarine under attack. We all just looked, and apart from Jimmy who went "Ha!" nobody dare say anything, but I could see Dad starting to shake.

Mam gave him a look and I heard something under the table, like somebody's leg being kicked. But Dad couldn't hold it in so he stuffed his napkin in his mouth just in time to stop a great big laugh. Unfortunately, the laugh came out of his nose, pushing a huge snotter in front of it.

Me and Jimmy howled and nearly wet our pants laughing. Well, I say nearly, but I think Jimmy actually did cos he got down from the table a minute later even though he had some pudding left. Mum just tutted and passed Dad a tea towel. Granny had missed it as she was pouring herself some more sherry.

Then, when Grandad got his breath back and stopped rubbing his ribs he said "Ey up lads, 'ere's another trick for ya!" and took his white linen napkin, still clean even at the end of the dinner, which was more than you could say for his sleeve, and hung it out flat in front of him. He showed us, the audience, both sides, "See there," he said, "a perfectly good napkin."

"An' it bloomin' well wants to be!" said Mam, "I paid five bob for the 'alf-dozen, mind you don't tear it!" But Grandad was flying off again into magic land. Me and Dad looked at each other, trying to remember if we'd seen this trick before, and we hadn't. Jimmy came back and climbed onto his chair.

"What you doing, Grandad?"

"Magic, me lad, just some good old-fashioned magic, watch this." He stuck up a finger on his right hand, and put the napkin over it, making it look like a tall, white rabbit ear. Then, with his left hand, he pretended to quickly pull a hair out of Granny's head, and didn't get told to bugger off because she was busy having a drink of her sherry, but she saw him out of her eye corner and sniffed real loud.

Then Grandad pretended to tie the invisible hair, a long one, around the top of the napkin and he pulled it back towards him. The ear twitched, just like he was really pulling it, and although I knew it was just his finger moving underneath, Jimmy thought it was real magic and his mouth was wide open, and with all the pudding he had stuck round his gob he looked like a chocolate doughnut.

Dad laughed a bit, but not cos he thought it was funny. Then Grandad, even though he's quite old, started to get excited. Mam would say he got carried away, and what happened next was a real surprise.

He took the napkin rabbit ear and pulled it through a hole he made in his left hand by putting his finger and thumb together. Then he got the lighted candle from the middle of the table and held it up so we could all see. Mam dropped her spoon into her dish with a clatter and Granny put her sherry glass back down. This was serious magic, and Dad winked at me. We'd certainly never seen this one before.

Then, with what I think you call a flourish, Grandad stuck the pointy bit of the napkin right into the flame and set it alight. Mam screamed and covered her mouth with her hands, probably to stop a lot of swearing coming out. Granny picked up her sherry glass and had another big drink while me and Dad and Jimmy just looked with our eyes as big as dinner plates.

The napkin was really burning now, with a big orange flame and smoke as black as coal going up to the ceiling and curling round the light bulb. Grandad laughed a bit, then spat in his other hand, but he didn't awk so it was just wet spit, then quick as a flash he grabbed at the flame and snuffed it out.

"Aha!" he said. There was still some smoke, though, and a bloomin' awful stink.

Mam looked a bit funny, like Jimmy looks when I've been spinning him round by his legs.

Granny put her glass down and without even looking reached across for the sherry bottle and got it first go. Dad looked like somebody had given him a good smack.

Meanwhile Grandad was rumpling the napkin up into a tight little ball and squashing it as small as he could into his hands, and laughing real loud. He was the only one laughing.

Me Dad was looking down at the table now, and Mam was staring up at the ceiling, shaking her head, saying some words very quietly. I'm fairly sure they were bad words.

And then, with the napkin completely scrunched up and hidden inside his gnarly old hands, more or less, Grandad got me to blow on them and say a magic word.

Abracadaver! I said, and he slowly peeked through the crack between his two thumbs, into the ball in his hands. Then he reached in with his teeth, pretending to pull really hard, and he groaned and growled a bit, and pulled out just a corner of the napkin. Slowly it all came out, and then quickly, with another big flourish he stretched out the napkin and held it up. He grinned and turned it around real proud like, showing us both sides, as if to say, "There, I bet you can't believe you saw this napkin on fire a minute ago!"

We all just stared.

Dad slowly closed his eyes. Jimmy had stopped breathing and I think he was trying real hard not to wet his pants again. Granny looked tired, like she does when she comes out of church, and she took another big drink of her sherry. Mam looked like she was going to be sick.

The napkin just hung there, with a great big burn hole right in the middle, and black marks coming out to the edges, like a big black spider with its guts shot out. I could see Grandad's face through the hole, peekaboo, and he was still smiling, the daft old beggar. I don't think he'd practised this one.

There was a pile of ash on Grandad's plate, making his pudding and white sauce look like a volcano, and his hands were all black. I suddenly heard the clock ticking, quite loud, on the sideboard. Funny how you notice things like that sometimes.

Nobody said anything, and I didn't think it was a very good trick. It smelled really bad. Nobody clapped but after a bit Dad said "Nice one, George."

Then Granny said something about going upstairs for a lie down, and took the sherry bottle with her. Dad suddenly remembered he still had the lights to get going so he went back into the living room, and Jimmy went with him to do his meddy evil fort.

Half a minute later it was just me, and Grandad and Mam sat at the kitchen table. But they weren't talking. Well, I think I heard Grandad say something, but it was just to himself, I think. Then I noticed it had stopped raining, so I grabbed me new bike and went outside. Enough magic for one day.

13

Down the Chimney

We had a new girl come to our school just before Christmas and teacher made her sit next to me, cos there was a spare seat. Her name was Sheila, and she was the only Sheila in our school so I never bothered to learn her last name. She smelled nice. She'd just moved here from somewhere over t'moors with her mother and they were living in the old blacksmith shop, right at the end of the village. It hadn't been a blacksmith's since Bodger's grandad died last year. He was the blacksmith. Well, he was til he died.

I remember Bodge telling me how he died. He was hammering a piece of red-hot iron to make a new hinge for the cemetery gate, cos the old one was broken. Some kids had been swinging on it, like we do, I mean like they do.

Anyway, he was hammering away at this hot iron and his cat, a black cat called Rivet, was chasing a mouse and it ran through his legs throwing him off balance and he hit himself on the head with the hammer. Knocked himself out, stone cold dead. Except for the hole in his head, which would be quite hot I suppose.

O'course, he was the next person through that cemetery gate and since he still hadn't mended the hinge the blokes carrying the coffin had a bit of a struggle. Me Mam said it was ironic, whatever that means. I just thought it was awkward. And they've left the gate like that ever since. The one hinge that's still on screeches like a scalded cat when you open it, but nobody swings on it anymore cos they say Bodge's grandad's ghost will come and get you and bang you on the head with his hammer.

So, anyway, the blacksmith's shop stopped being a blacksmith's shop and Bodge's dad did some alterations to make it into a cottage. Well, he just dragged out all the tools and scrap metal and swept up and Bodge's mam cleaned the windows. Snack Waudby, who's a plumber, put a toilet in and a kitchen sink, and they found some bits o'furniture and a few pots and pans. The blacksmith's anvil was too heavy to shift so they put a cushion on it and called it a stool. They put a folding screen around the toilet and hung a curtain across to divide the bedroom from the other part, which was everything else, and that was it.

Renovated. They called it Blacksmith's Cottage and made a sign for it spelled out of old horseshoe nails. I thought our house was rough but this was like indoor camping. With free soot. Mam said it was the only cottage in the village where you wiped your feet when you came out, not when you went in.

They used the old forge as a fireplace and it had a great big wide chimney. Bodge said he'd climbed right up it once, from the inside. He said it was easy cos it was so wide. And I remember me Dad telling me how they used to send young boys up chimneys to clean 'em. He threatened to send me up ours when I did ought bad.

Anyway, Bodge had climbed up then he'd sat on the roof, feeding the crows with some old biscuit crumbs out of his pocket. He said you could see all sorts from up there. But happen he didn't see Constable Wiggle come up the street who tried to arrest him for mischief. Bodge got off by saying he was just cleaning the chimney for his dad. He probably looked like he had anorl cos he's always black mucky is Bodge.

Thing is, I liked this Sheila. I never told her, o'course. I never mentioned it to anybody. But she was nice and she told me how they hadn't got much money. She said her dad had left her mam and ran off with another woman who only had one leg. I don't know how they managed that but I didn't like to ask.

She said they had no Christmas tree or lights or decorations and she wasn't expecting Father Christmas to come on Christmas Eve, which was a real shame, I thought, seeing as how they had the biggest, widest chimney in the village. I felt a bit sorry for her, not that we had much either, but I wanted to give her a Christmas present, summat for her to open. Mind, I didn't want her to know it was from me. I didn't want anybody to know. But I had no money to buy owt, and she certainly wouldn't want summat I'd made, like a slingshot or a mouse trap. Or you never know, maybe she would... Then I suddenly had an idea.

Last year for Christmas me Aunt Dorothy sent me a homemade scarf and it was awful. I hated it. It wasn't scratchy like most of 'em are. It was quite soft and warm. But it was bright pink. She'd made me Mam a cardigan in the same colour so I reckon she just had some bloomin' wool left over that she wanted rid of. Me Mam said it's the thought that counts and I said well what was she thinking of then? Anyway, a pink scarf would be just the job for Sheila. I'd only worn it once and then I told me Mam I lost it, but I'd just hidden it inside one of me Dad's wellies, the old ones in the shed that he never wears.

So, after school, when Jimmy had gone to watch rabbits in the back field and I had the house to meself, I went and got the scarf. There was some mouse poo on it but it was dry and it brushed off. I wanted to wrap it up for her but I didn't know where me Mam had put the wrapping paper, if we had any. Or the sticky tape. So I got some newspaper and then I found some string to tie it up with. I'd taken the string off a parcel of meat in the pantry, and it had some blood on, but I thought the red would look Christmasy.

I found one of Jimmy's crayons on the floor, a green one, and I drew a few holly leaves on the newspaper to brighten it up. I tried drawing a reindeer but it looked more like a holly leaf than me holly leaves did. I wrote her name on in crayon, and finally, it was ready. Next problem was how to get it to her. For now, I hid it back in me Dad's welly and put a sack over it to keep the mice out.

I knew Sheila didn't go straight home from school cos she said she went to the shop where her mam worked, and helped her in the back, weighing apples, washing eggs, and bagging up flour. She said they didn't like her mam upfront serving customers cos she swore a lot. Well, maybe it makes you swear when your husband runs off with a one-legged woman.

I thought real hard and came up with a plan. If I nipped home after school and got the present while she was at the shop, I could run it round to Blacksmith's Cottage and leave it there for her to find.

I'd do this last day of school, the day before Christmas Eve. Bodge said there was always a key for the door hidden under a bucket behind a little holly bush. I'd let meself in and put the present under the Christmas tree. If they'd managed to get one. Sheila said they weren't having much for Christmas cos her mam was broke. Anyway, I'd leave it somewhere for her to find. Maybe put it on the hearth and leave a note. No. Not leave a note. Say nowt, just leave it. Father Christmas can take the credit.

Finally, last day of school came and the teacher seemed real happy and said Merry Christmas to each of us as we got our coats on and left by the front door. I wandered about a bit then walked over to the kerb where Sheila was waiting to cross the road. I tried to act all casual. "You off to the shop, then?" I said.

She jumped a bit but when she saw it was me she smiled. "Yes, I am. Merry Christmas, Derek. I hope you have a nice time." I smiled back at her. Least, I think I did. Then I turned and ran up the street to our house.

I got the present and tucked it under me coat and set off back towards Blacksmith's Cottage. I was real excited. This was going to be an adventure! A secret adventure. No, a *Top Secret* adventure! I never saw anybody on the way there, which was good, cos you have to be very careful on *Top Secret* adventures, and it was starting to get dark which helped. Street was quiet. I slowed down when I got near the cottage. There were no lights on and I knocked on the door just to make sure there was nobody in. And there wasn't.

I went across and looked for the bucket behind the holly bush. I pricked meself loads of times but I daren't make a noise so I just swore inside me head. I think our teacher does that. I know me Dad does when Mam's listening. I finally found the bucket and looked underneath. No key! I looked all round the bush, crawling about on me hands and knees, feeling among the weeds and wet grass. And I think I smelled some dog muck, but no bloomin' key! How was I going to get in?

I stood up and went over and tried the window. Locked. Same with the window at the back anorl. Bugger. Then... I remembered the chimney! If Bodge could climb up and down it then so could I. I wasn't as fat as him.

There was a barrel next to the coalhouse wall, and the coalhouse was built up against the side of the cottage. If I got on the barrel, then onto the coalhouse roof I could get onto the cottage roof, then pop down the chimney, leave the present and pop back up again, smartish. This *Top Secret* adventure was getting even better!

I made sure the present was well tucked in and me jacket all fastened up to keep it there. Then I got up on the barrel, then onto the coalhouse, then onto the cottage roof. Easy! I walked across the tiles to the chimney, and it was a bit slape cos of all the moss, but I got got there and stood on me tiptoes and looked in.

It was plenty wide, like Bodge said it was, but it looked a bit dark. I scrambled up and sat on the top with me legs dangling down into it. I was a bit scared.

Alright then, I was a lot scared. They never seem to look scared when you see 'em do *Top Secret* stuff on the telly, do they?

It's now or never, I said, and shuffled off me bum and grabbed the top of the chimney with both hands and slowly lowered meself down. The chimney walls were quite rough so it was easy to get a foothold, but the soot made it a bit slippery. Down I went, holding on with me fingers til me foot found a hold. Then down another step. I thought I was going to sneeze cos of the soot but I didn't.

It was getting lighter as I looked down and soon I was just above the hearth. I thought I could drop down the last bit, and so I did. There was a big rustle and a crunch. Like newspaper being scrunched up and twigs snapping. Turns out that's what it was. Somebody had laid the fire out ready to light with paper and kindling, and I'd squashed it flat. Never mind.

I stepped out into the room and looked about. It was gloomy. I couldn't see a tree or much of anything. It smelled of onions. Then I saw two little lights come out from under the table. It was like eyes. Ghostly eyes! It was a ghost! Bodge's grandad was coming at me! He was mad at me for breaking in! *This was too much adventure now!* The eyes got closer and closer then, just as me heart stopped, I heard "Miaow!" I didn't know they had a bloomin' cat! Sheila never said. I shoocd it away. I've always liked dogs better.

The fireplace hearth was all mucky with ashes and soot so I thought I'd best leave the present somewhere else. I couldn't see any Christmas stockings hung anywhere. It didn't look a bit like Christmas at all. There was a big curtain hung down, halfway across the room. I looked behind and there were two small beds. One had an old teddy bear on it so I knew that must be Sheila's. I put the present under her pillow and went back across to the hearth.

It was fairly dark now and I banged into the bloomin' anvil stool thing and hurt me knee. Ow! But I knew I hadn't time to sit down and rub it. I had to get out. Back up that bloomin' chimney. Mind, climbing up wasn't as easy as climbing down. Specially with a bad knee. It took me ages just to get halfway. Then I heard something. Voices. I could hear voices. Outside. Sheila's voice and somebody else. Her mam. Then I heard a key go into the lock. Oh no, they'd come home! Me *Top Secret* adventure didn't look like it was going to be a secret much longer.

I heard the door creak open and Sheila's mam say "Come on love, let's get that fire lit and warm the place up." You what? They can't light the bloody fire with me stuck in here! What am I gonna do? Should I tell 'em? What could I say? Maybe I could say Bodge asked me come and clean the chimney for 'em. No. Stupid!

I started to climb up again, a bit faster but trying not to make a row and knock any soot down. I felt all prickly under me arms and I started to sweat a bit. I couldn't find any rough bits on the chimney to put me feet on and I kept slippin' on the soot.

I heard Sheila's mam fluffing up the newspaper and sorting the twigs out in the grate just below me. She said a bad word. Then I heard her rattle a box of matches. No! I was scrambling at the walls now but getting nowhere. Me knee was killing me and I couldn't get a grip. Sheila's mam struck a match. I heard it scrape on the matchbox. I'm dead, I thought. I have to shout down and tell 'em I'm up here. But I daren't. I couldn't. *I was going to burn to death! No!*

I remember me Dad's mate at the fire station saying that most people in a fire don't die from burning, they die from the smoke. Well, maybe they do, but that wasn't much bloody comfort to me right now.

I heard her strike another match. Then another. She couldn't get 'em going. I could hear her getting mad and she said a few more bad words and threw the box into the fireplace. "Sheila?" she said, "The cat's pissed on the matches again! Can you run down the shop and get some more?"

Oh, glad tidings of great joy that was! I had a few more minutes now to get meself out. I started climbing up again, an inch at a time, trying not to make a sound. I heard Sheila getting some money from her mam and then zipping her coat up. A few more grabs and climbs and I was up on the roof. I was out o'breath and gasping in the cold night air. It was dark. Stars were coming out. I could smell the smoke from other people's chimneys in the village.

I slid down the tiles to the coalhouse roof, with a bit of a clatter cos of the moss, then I struggled down to the edge on me bum, turned round, and felt for the barrel with me feet. I couldn't find the bloomin' thing so I dangled off the guttering for a bit... struggling... then knew I just had to drop to the ground. Me knee just gave way when I landed and I crumpled into a heap on the wet grass. *Ow!*

What a miserable bloomin' adventure this had turned out. *Top Secrets* are never as good as you think they're going to be. And this bloomin' *Top Secret* was turning out to be a Bottom Secret. And it was my bottom that would be feelin' it if me Mam and Dad found out. I rocked backwards and forwards, rubbing me knee and sayin' the same bad words I'd heard Sheila's mam say.

"Who's there?" said a voice, and Sheila stepped round the corner and shone a torch on me. "Oh, it's you Derek? What on earth are you doing down there?" I've hurt me knee, I said. I was, er, I was taking a shortcut and fell over a brick. Sheila shone her torch around the ground, at t'front and behind me, and saw there was a real shortage of bricks.

Well anyway, I said, getting up on me feet, I'd best be getting back home for me tea. She shone the torch up and down me. "Why are you all black?" she said. Me? Black? Am I? I wasn't when I left home.

"Yes," she said, and laughed, "You look like a chimney sweep!" Oh right, yeah. Well, I've been, er, trying to catch a rat in me Aunt Mary's coalhouse. In t'dark. Without a torch. It was a real struggle. Mucky job.

She laughed again, "I bet that was an adventure." Oh aye, I said, I like adventures, me. Usually. Some of 'em. Anyway, I should be getting off. Don't want to miss Father Christmas tonight, do we, eh?

"Hmm, I think he might have already been," she said. I thought, aye, maybe he has been, but it's a good thing he didn't bring your mam some dry matches. I couldn't see her face in the dark but it sounded like she was smiling. Right then, I said, goodnight. I was set to go but she stepped in front of me.

"Ee, Derek. You can't go home looking like that," she said, "Come here." And she whipped out a hankie, spat on it, then grabbed me jacket and pulled me towards her. She was real strong. A lot stronger than she looked. With the hankie in one hand and the torch in the other she wiped round me eyes, then me cheeks, and then me chin. She finally wiped round me mouth, each lip, real careful and slow...

"There, that's a bit better," and she smiled, and turned the torch off. It went all quiet. Then she kissed me. On the lips. Just like that. Without even asking. A great big kiss. Seemed to last ages. I mean, it was all very nice, but if anything wanted kissing it was me bloody knee. Mind, it was nice. Right nice. Felt grand. Took me mind off me knee. Took me mind off Christmas... and everything else anorl.

She turned the torch back on, stepped away and pulled her coat collar up. "Brr, it's cold tonight, eh? Merry Christmas, Derek. I have to go to the shop and get matches now."

As she walked away I was going to say What you need is a nice warm scarf, young lady! But I couldn't move me mouth.

DAVE PRESTON

14

Awake in a Manger

It was the night before the night before Christmas. Christmas Eve Eve, maybe, but I've never heard anyone call it that. Anway, we were all in t'kitchen. Mam was cooking summat, and our Jimmy was colouring a picture of Father Christmas, but he'd run out of red. And patience. I was looking at last week's comic, again, cos I didn't get one this week. Spent me pocket money on a present for Mam instead.

Me Dad had given up on the Christmas tree lights, as usual, and was trying to get the little plastic toys back in the Christmas crackers. See, me and Jimmy had found the crackers in the cupboard under the stairs and we worked out how to open 'em up without pulling 'em. It was easy really. Any road, we'd left the hats alone and the jokes were rubbish, but we larked with the little toys for a bit, but forgot to put 'em back. Me Dad would have got real mad usually, but Mam said Christmas was enough of a strain without him turning his 'og out.

There was a knock at the back door. Mam opened it and there was Uncle Arthur, stood there in his wellies and mucky overalls. He's not really me uncle. He's one of dozens I have. I think they're just friends with Mam and Dad, but we call 'em uncle. I have loads of Aunties anorl.

Anyway, me Mam say "Hello Arthur, come in!" and he does, then sits down at t'kitchen table, with me Dad. He rubbed his hand on top of me head as he went past and messed me hair up. Why do uncles do that? He usually brings us eggs but not tonight.

"Now then, Arthur, what's up?" says Dad, "You look worried to death."

"Aye," said Uncle Arthur, very quietly. I could 'ardly 'ear 'im. "It's Peggy. They say she hasn't got long now."

I think he meant me Aunt Peggy, Uncle Arthur's sister, who lives in York. I know she's been poorly for ages, since last Christmas. Me Mam and Dad always talk about her in whispers, the way grownups do when even they don't want to hear what they're saying, never mind us kids. They were talking like that now. Uncle Arthur whispered summat about going to see her tomorrow but he was right worried about one of his pigs farrowing. Dad whispered summat back, and Mam kept looking over at us, and me and Jimmy pretended we weren't listening. Well, I know Jimmy wasn't cos he'd packed in crayoning and was reading a book from school. Summat about leaving a candle in the window at Christmas.

"Cup o'tea, Arthur, love, or summat a bit stronger?" said Mam?

"Summat a lot stronger," said Dad, and he got up and went into the pantry. He came out with a green bottle that had two little dogs on t'label. One black and one white. Whisky, I think, and he poured Uncle Arthur a big glass. And then he poured one for himself. Mam looked through t'kitchen window and whispered again, but just to herself.

They clinked their glasses and had a sip. A big sip. Then Dad said "Look, Arthur, just you let us know what needs doing."

"Well I'm hoping to be on t'first train in t'morning," said Uncle Arthur, so I'll fother up early. But it's Mary I'm worried over."

"Mary?" said Mam.

"Aye, Mary, me champion Landrace. She's due to farrow any minute. I should be there now, but..."

I know what farrowing means. It's when a pig has babies. I've seen it meself. They have a real bright, red lamp hung over 'em to keep 'em all warm. I like seeing baby piglets. They're all pink and soft.

"Aye," said Dad, "Well, I know me way round your spot, so I'll fother up if you're not there."

"She's in that little stable next to t'barn, and there's a pig lamp on her and plenty o'bedding. You know where all t'feed is, right? And there's bottles in t'dairy if she has a runt that needs milk. Look, I'll do me best but if I can't get back tomorrow night you'll see to Mary, as well as all t'other lot?"

T'other lot meant a load of hens, a few ducks, two geese, and four sheep. As well as the two pigs. Uncle Arthur got rid of his cows ages ago cos he didn't like milking 'em. Oh, and there's an old donkey anorl, that he said was good for nowt but didn't have the heart to get rid of. We called it Stinky, cos Uncle Arthur gives it onions to eat and they make it fart. A lot.

Anyway, it was a grand little farm and me Dad used to go and help out. Quite a bit, lately. Especially when Mam had too many jobs for him at home. We always had fun larking round there. I never knew the animals had names, though. Barry Tate at school lives on a farm and he's not allowed to give the animals names. His dad says there's no point getting friendly with 'em cos they all end up dead in t'pantry.

Uncle Arthur finally got up and left, after finishing his whisky and after giving Mam a big kiss and shaking me Dad's hand for what seemed like ages. I heard him make Dad promise to look after things til he got back from York. Mind, if he knew what me Dad's promises were like he coulda saved his breath.

"I like ord Arthur," said me Dad, after he closed the door. "You know where you stand with 'im."

"Aye," said Mam, "a long way off and preferably downwind."

Then they started whisperin' and looking at t'clock, and then at me and Jimmy, then at t'clock again.

"It'll be right," said me Dad. "Come on, let's have a sit down in t'other room while I finish me drink." And they both went into t'front room.

"Hey Der, I'm going to have a candle in the window on Christmas Eve," said Jimmy. "I am, just like in this here story."

What you on about? I said.

"See," said Jimmy, "This family hadn't got much money but they knew there were people out and about on cold days and nights who had even less, so they put a candle in the window to let travellers know they were welcome to come in for a warm."

Who's going to see a candle in our kitchen window? I said.

"Ah, well, see I've thought about that," said Jimmy, "so I'm going to put it in *t'front* room window, so they can all see it from t'street."

Where you getting t'candle? I said.

"Got one!" said Jimmy. "I swapped a Mars bar for it after school wi' Dennis Brown."

What Mars bar? I said. Not... not that one that was behind the bread bin in t'pantry was it?

Jimmy looked away and started flicking through the pages in his book.

That was *my* Mars bar! I said. I've been saving it! You owe me!

"All I need is a nice bottle to put it in," said Jimmy. "And I know where I can get one."

Mam and Dad were still in the front room and I could hear them talkin quietly. I think they were a bit upset that Dad was going to be at the farm on

Christmas Eve and miss out on what we did at home. Which was usually a lot of shouting and being told off.

We had to go to bed early that night but in the morning Jimmy was up first and was rattling about down in the pantry, even before Mam got up.

We all had our breakfast at t'kitchen table, which wasn't what we usually did, but Mam was telling us we had to be extra good because Dad might not be there for most of the day, especially if Mary had her piglets.

Can I come with yer, Dad? I said, I can help fother up. "Nay lad," said me Dad, "You'll be needed round here to help your Mother. There's coal to bring in, fire's to mend, and baking to put away, and if you're real good you can have a go at them Christmas lights. There's spare bulbs in that shoebox under t'stairs."

He didn't usually let me play with electric stuff so I knew he was trying to stop me from moaning. Mind, Jimmy was doing enough moaning for both of us.

"Well, maybe let's all of us go with you at first and have a look at the farm," said Mam. "We could all use some fresh air." Then she made Dad some samwidges and put 'em in an old OXO tin. "And you'll be wanting a drink," she said. "Oh, I'll take me flask," said Dad.

We all put our coats on, and got gloves and hats. Jimmy put his school shoes on and started trying to tie the laces. "No, not school shoes!" said Mam. "It's a bloomin' farm! What are you thinking, lad?" So we put our wellies on and finally got set off.

"Looks like snow," said Dad. And it was a bit dark, even if it was still morning.

On the way past t'village green we saw the big wooden star that the vicar had put up. Well, actually, Geoffrey Simpson put it up cos t'vicar's useless. It had lights on but they weren't workin'. And underneath it were two big letters cut out o'plywood and painted white. Well, whiteish. *JO*, it said.

"Who the 'eck's *JO*?" said Jimmy. That's Mary's husband, *JO*, I said. His real name's Joseph but his mates call him *JO*. I was making this up.

"It's supposed to say JOY," said Mam, "but everybody knows that doesn't last long round 'ere. Somebody's probably nicked it for firewood."

We got to Uncle Arthur's and went into the farmyard through t'big gate. Some hens ran over to meet us but we had nowt to give 'em so they soon lost interest and went back to scratchin' around in t'muck.

"Right," said Dad, "She'll be over here," and he led us over to a stable door. The top half of the door was open, so he looked in over the top. "She's not farrowed yet," he whispered.

Mam looked a bit disappointed cos once a pig's farrowed and all t'piglets are settled down you can leave 'em be. But until t'piglets are born you have to keep an eye on things, so Dad would be here for quite a bit.

"Can we see, Dad?" said Jimmy, and Dad opened the bottom half of the door and we looked in. Mary was lying down over in the corner on some straw, and the pig lamp was shining down. Looked real cosy.

"Right then, let's leave your Dad to it. Do you have everything you need, love?"

"Aye," said Dad, "I'll be grand. I have me sandwiches and me flask. I'll try and get back soon as I can. He gave Mam a quick kiss. "Right then, you lads be good for your Mother or I'll be telling Father Christmas! He always has room on his Naughty List for a few more."

"He could fill it twice over from this village," said Mam.

So we left me Dad there and went home. By the time I'd brought the coal in, swept the hearth, put two dozen mince pies in a tin, and helped Mam fettle the Christmas dinner and tidy up, it was getting dark. I had a go at t'Christmas lights. Half the bulbs were out so I unscrewed a few and put some new ones in, but they didn't look new. By the end of it less than half were lit so I just chucked 'em all back on the Christmas tree and didn't turn 'em back on. That way you couldn't see if they were working or not. We could pretend they were.

Jimmy had also been helping Mam put the Christmas baking away but by the look of the mess under his chair at t'kitchen table he'd been putting some of it away in his gob.

Mam kept looking at the clock and tutting. "Your Dad's not going to be home in time for his tea," she said. But he took some grub with him, I said. He'll be alright.

So we had our teas and there was more to go round without Dad there. I had three sausages all to meself, and extra toast. We usually just have beans and toast on Christmas Eve but this year we had sausages as well, for a treat. I think it's cos that's what they had in the Bible before Jesus was born.

After tea, Jimmy kept nagging Mam to light his candle in the front window. It was stuck in the neck of a bottle with two little dogs on. Black and White.

Mam asked him where he'd got the candle and the bottle but she didn't wait for answer. She just lit the candle, told us not to mess with it, and went back to the kitchen.

"Looks good, eh, Derek?" said Jimmy. Aye, I said, Well done. But where d'you get the bottle? Didn't that have Dad's whisky in it a bit back?

"It's alright, Der, I saved the whisky." Mind, it did look nice in the window, shining bright and cheerful. I did wonder what would happen if a hungry traveller came knocking at the door, though. I suppose Mam would have to see to that.

Then we watched a Christmas film and then some people singing carols outside a church, then a vicar talking for ages about the miracle of Christmas, but he never mentioned Father Christmas, and when you think about it he works some fairly useful miracles on Christmas Eve. He could give Jesus a run for his money.

Mam was getting a bit het up. She was in and out of the kitchen and front room then up and down stairs, chuntering away to herself. Finally she came in and turned the telly off. "Right. Get your coats and wellies on. We're off to see what's going on at that farm." It was about bedtime but we didn't argue.

So a few minutes later were were marching down the village to Uncle Arthur's. It was real dark now so we kept to the side where the streetlights were.

"Ey look!" said Jimmy, pointing up to a streetlight.

"It's snowin'! Look it's snowing'!" By gum, I said, It is anorl! Mam didn't seem bothered.

"Come on," she said, "Let's just get there and see if your Dad's alright."

She struggled a bit with the big gate latch but we finally got in. The farmyard was mostly dark and quiet. All the animals would be asleep, I thought. Then we walked slowly over to where there was some light coming out of the little stable. Mam quietly opened the top half of the door and looked in. "Oh my lord..." she said. What Mam? I said, What is it? What?

"Right, be quiet," she whispered, "and we'll sneak in. Slowly. And not a word." She quietly opened the bottom door and me and Jimmy crowded into the doorway next to her. Over in the corner under the red pig lamp was Mary, sort of sleeping, but grunting a bit every now and then. And sprawled all over her were a mass of pink piglets, all jostling about and trying get to her teats, cos that's where the milk comes from. Well, half the piglets were crawling all over

Mary, and the other half were crawling all over Dad, who was lying next to her. Asleep. He was snoring. The empty OXO tin was on the straw, and next to that was his flask. It was all lovely to look at, all warm and cuddly.

Jimmy crept up to Dad, and reached down for the flask. He looked real worried.

What's up? I whispered. Mam was busy wiping her nose with a hankie. And her eyes.

"It's the flask," said Jimmy. "That's where I put the stuff out of the bottle with the two dogs."

Great! So Dad had drunk a flask full of whisky. Or spilt it. No, the straw was dry so I'm fairly sure he must have drunk it. I thought about telling Mam, but then thought again. Me Dad often says "Let sleeping dogs lie." And I think this was one of them times to let 'em lie. So I did.

Then we heard a big fart. I looked straight away at Jimmy, and he was looking at me. We didn't look at Mam cos she never does that. And then we got the smell... Ugh! It was bloody awful! It started to make me eyes water. Mam covered her mouth and nose with the hankie. I think she said "Oh good lord!" or summat like that. Then out of the darkness at the other corner of the stable we heard a rustle in the straw. And there looking at us was Stinky, the donkey. He seemed to be smiling, well pleased with himself.

"Right," said Mam, "I think we've seen enough," and she reached down and shook me Dad by the shoulder and tried to wake him up, but he was dead to the world.

"Never mind," she said, "He must be tired out after helping her deliver all these piglets, poor man. Best leave him." But it's Christmas Eve, Mam!" I said.

"He'll come home when he's ready," she said. "We won't have Christmas without him, he knows that."

I couldn't wait to get home. I was a bit worried we'd missed Father Christmas. I was wondering if he'd already been and saw the house was empty, so he'd just buggered off somewhere else. We'd never been out this late on a Christmas Eve. Father Christmas would be real busy. He wouldn't have time to 'ang about waiting for us to get back.

While we were walking home I heard Mam ask Jimmy again about where he got the bottle and the candle. When he mentioned about the Mars bar she looked at me and shook her head. Then when he told her about getting the bottle and using the flask...she grabbed us both by the hands and picked up the pace. Not another word was said, and we soon got across the village to our house. We went through t'front gate and up the path.

"Look Mam!" said Jimmy, "Me candle's still going!"

And it was. We got right up to the front window, and stopped, all three of us staring at it. There wasn't a lot of candle left. Then, just as we watched, the flame seemed to cough, then it got bigger for just a second, then it went out. Gone. Just some white smoke curlin' up, like summat sinking, but upside down.

"Right, you two," said Mam, "*IN!*"

Father Christmas Suppers

It's nice to leave old Father Christmas a little something nice for him to eat and drink on Christmas Eve.

He works very hard and deserves a snack or two to keep his energy up. As the wise old man in Chapter 4 told us, depending on the Christmas Eve weather, Father Christmas prefers certain snacks being left out for him when he visits your home.

If it's **frosty** ~ a glass of rum, three crackers, and a knob of cheese.

If it's **snowing** ~ a glass of brandy, a sausage roll, and a chocolate biscuit.

If it's **mild** ~ a glass of milk and three digestive biscuits.

If it's **windy** ~ a glass of whisky and a small pork pie.

If it's **raining** ~ a glass of sherry and three chocolate biscuits.

If it's **foggy** ~ a glass of port and a sausage roll.

(You can also leave something he can give to his reindeer. They love carrots!)

Bradley Christmas Recipes

The following recipes come from traditional Yorkshire kitchens, including Derek's, and are guaranteed to give winter hunger a right good seeing to. They are not guaranteed to help you lose weight or stay slim, but Christmas is not a time to worry about that.

Many chefs and cooks treat their recipes like scientific formulae and insist on following every measurement and instruction to the letter. These recipes are not like that. It's quite alright to muck about and add a bit of whatever you fancy. Just like when the Bradleys concocted that wonderful Wassail brew! Let the spirit of Christmas guide you.

Where possible, buy fresh and support your local farmers and growers. If you haven't got good company in the kitchen, at least put on some good music, and please share whatever comes out of the oven, especially with those less fortunate than you.

Since these stories are from the Bradley family of the 1960s, the recipe measurements are as well. There was no metric in their old kitchen.

Dad's Big Mince Pie

One unbaked pie crust of choice, enough dough for a bottom and a top
4 apples, cored and diced
½ cup raisins
1/3 cup apple juice
1 orange, scrubbed, juiced, and the peel grated (use both the juice and the grated peel)
¾ cup brown sugar
½ teaspoon cinnamon
½ teaspoon cloves

Preheat oven to 400F. Place all ingredients (except pie crust) in a saucepan and simmer over medium heat, stirring occasionally, for 10-15 minutes until apples begin to soften.

Pour filling into unbaked pie crust shell. Roll second piece of dough out and cut into strips 1/2"wide. Weave strips over top of pie to make a lattice crust. (You could omit this step and cut out decorative shapes from the dough instead, placing them around the top of the pie.) Bake for 40 minutes, covering lightly with aluminum foil if crust starts to burn. Dad tries to eat this all by himself, but he always shares it in the end.

Jimmy's Little Brandy Snaps

2 oz butter
1 level teaspoon ground ginger
2 oz sugar
1 teaspoon brandy
2 tablespoons golden syrup
¼ teaspoon grated lemon rind
2 oz flour

Melt the fat, sugar and syrup in a pan. Remove from the heat and add the other ingredients. Mix well. Drop teaspoonfuls of the mixture onto a greased baking sheet, about 3 inches apart. Bake for 7 to 10 minutes in a moderate oven. Remove the sheet from the oven and let it stand for a moment on the top of the stove until a biscuit will lift up when a knife is inserted underneath. Roll the biscuits one at a time round the handle of a wooden spoon, leave a minute to set, then slide off. Fill with piped whipped cream and leave in the fridge until serving. They might be little, but they're a big hit with Jimmy.

Derek's Favourite Cheesecake

9 oz shortcrust pastry

Filling:

2 oz butter

2 oz caster sugar

12 oz cottage cheese, sieved

2 medium eggs, beaten

3 oz raisins

Grated rind and juice of one lemon

2 oz ground almonds

Roll out the pastry and line an 8-inch loose bottomed or spring form deep flan ring. Chill in the refrigerator. Heat the oven to 375 F. Make the filling by creaming together the butter and the sugar and gradually adding the cheese. Stir in the remaining in gradients and mix thoroughly. Spoon this into the pastry case, stand on a baking tray and cook in the oven for approximately 40 minutes until the filling is just set. If possible remove the sides from the flan ring and return to the oven for 10 minutes to ensure that the pastry sides are well cooked. Leave to cool and serve cold. Derek says he could live on this. For a day, at least.

Mam's Cut-and-Come-Again Cake

8 oz SR flour

4 oz sugar

4 oz butter

6 oz mixed fruit

½ teaspoon salt

1 teaspoon mixed spice

2 oz glace cherries

2 oz chopped nuts

1 egg

7 tablespoons milk

Put flour, sugar, spice, salt, in bowl rub in margarine lightly.

Add fruit etc.

Beat eggs in milk and add to mixture, mix well, to dropping consistency.

Grease and line a 2 lb loaf tin.

Oven temperature 375o Reg 4.

Bake for about 80 minutes or until well risen and golden brown.

Mam likes to serve this with a good strong cup of Orange Pekoe tea.

Granny's Festive Fruit Loaf

8 oz butter

8 oz currants

7 oz sugar

2 oz mixed peel

3 eggs, beaten

1 ¼ lb self-raising flour

2 tablespoons golden syrup

¼ pint of milk

8oz sultanas

½ teaspoon bicarbonate of soda

Cream the butter and sugar, add the beaten eggs, then the warmed syrup. Add the fruit, then the flour, alternating with milk in which the bicarbonate of soda has been dissolved. Pour into 2 large, greased loaf tins, and bake in a moderate oven for 90 minutes. This cake keeps a while and will get better. If you are going to keep it, Granny suggests you keep it moist with a drop of good sherry every now and again.

Grandad Bradley's Perfect Parkin

1 lb. fine oatmeal

½ tsp bicarbonate soda

1 lb dark treacle

2 tbsp demarara sugar

¼ lb butter

1 tbsp milk

½ oz ginger

Rub butter into oatmeal, add ginger and sugar.

Melt treacle.

Dissolve soda in milk.

Mix everything together.

Line baking tin with well greased paper and pour in mixture.

Bake in a low to moderate oven for 30-45 minutes. Don't cut it until it's cool.

Grandad says that if you make it just right you can dunk it in your tea.

The Bradley Pork Pie

Pastry: 8 oz plain flour

3 oz lard or pork fat

1 teaspoon salt

½ pint of milk

2 egg yolks

Filling: 12 oz lean pork (ground or small pieces)

Salt and pepper

½ teaspoon mixed herbs

pinch salt

pinch mace

¼ pint of jellied stock (1 teaspoon of gelatin & a stock cube)

Chop pork finely and season. Mix flour and salt in a bowl. Bring milk and fat to a boil in a saucepan and pour onto flour. Add one egg yolk mix up quickly and knead. Mould into baking pan while still warm, leaving 1/3 of pastry for the lid.

Fill pan with chopped pork etc and make the pastry lid with your hands (not with a roller) save a small knob for holly leaves. Make a hole in the center of the lid with a wooden spoon handle. Form the knob of pastry into two holly leaves and decorate the lid.

Baking:

Put a greaseproof collar around the tin and place on middle shelf in the oven pre-heated to 475F for 20 minutes. Turn down to 375F and bake for ninety minutes. Take greaseproof cover off tin and brush the second egg yolk, mixed with a little milk, onto the lid. Return to oven for 40 minutes. Remove and let cool in tin. Make jellied stock with hot water, gelatin and stock cube, bring to the boil and pour into pie through the center hole. Let cool.

Note: whole, shelled, hardboiled eggs can be added to the pork filling before baking. Place them along the middle of the pan, halfway up the filling, completely surrounded by pork filling. Serve with pickled onions, HP or tomato sauce, and chutney (or *Branston Pickle*). If it's cold out side Dad has a dash of hot mustard with it.

Dad's Quick Ginger Beer

Mix together:

2 gallons boiling water

2 oz well-bruised ginger root

2 sliced lemons

2 teaspoons cream of tartar

2 lb sugar

Stir well until all the sugar is dissolved and when cold add 1oz fresh brewer's yeast spread on a piece of toast.

Let it work in a warm place (covered) for 24 hours, then strain and bottle.

If it's giving you a lovely warm feeling, you made it right. Cheers!

Mam's Rhubarb Chutney

4 lb rhubarb trimmed and cut into small pieces

1 lb onions, skinned and diced

2 lb demerara sugar

1 lb raisins

2 teaspoons ground ginger

2 teaspoons curry powder

1 ½ pints malt vinegar

Place the rhubarb, onion, sugar, raisins, spices and ½ pint of the vinegar in a large, heavy based saucepan and cook gently until the rhubarb is soft and tender. Add the rest of the vinegar and continue cooking steadily, stirring occasionally until of a thick consistency. Pot in warm, clean jars and cover. Mam says it goes with almost anything (except Turkish Delight).

Bradley Christmas Pudding & Brandy Sauce

8 oz Currants

4 oz Sultanas

4 oz Raisins

4 oz Chopped candied peel

1 oz Skinned chopped almonds

4 oz Wholewheat flour

½ tsp Salt

½ tsp Grated nutmeg

½ tsp Ground ginger

1 ½ tsp Mixed spice

8 oz Brown sugar

4 oz Wholewheat breadcrumbs

8 oz Vegetable suet

1 Lemon, juice rind

1 tbsp Molasses

5 tbsp Water rum mixed

Grease a 2-pint pudding basin use a large saucepan to hold the basin. Wash currants, sultanas raisins in warm water pat dry. Put fruit in large bowl with candied peel almonds. Sift flour, salt spices into bowl add sugar, breadcrumbs suet.

Mix well then stir in lemon juice, rind molasses with enough of the water rum mixture to make a soft mixture. Turn into the basin, cover with waxed paper aluminum foil put basin into pot. Pour enough water into the pot to reach halfway up the side of the basin. Bring to a boil, cover saucepan let pudding steam gently for 4 hours, watching the water level topping up with boiling water if necessary. When cooked, cool the pudding store in a cool dry place for up to 2 months.

Before serving, steam pudding again for 3 hours. Turn out onto a serving platter flame with brandy if you desire.

If preferred, divide the pudding in half making two smaller puddings. Keeps up to 3 months in the fridge.

To serve it just like Mam does, you bury a threepenny piece inside – but warn folks in case they bite down on it and lose a filling!

Bradley Curd Tart

Pastry:

4 oz plain flour

1 oz icing sugar

2 oz butter

½ beaten egg

Curd:

3 pts milk (not skimmed)

fresh lemon juice (1 lemon)

4 oz butter

1 ½ beaten eggs

cinnamon, nutmeg

To make pastry:

Mix flour and sugar and rub in butter.

Add beaten egg and mix.

To make curd: Heat the milk almost to boiling, add lemon juice and stir until it curdles. Allow to stand until cool, and drain through a cheesecloth overnight. This should produce about 10 oz of curd.

Beat the butter. Mix in the curds. Mix in the beaten eggs, then grate in cinnamon to taste. Line an 8" tin with pastry, fill with mix, sprinkle with nutmeg, and bake at 190oC for 25-30 minutes. If you prefer, you can add a handful of currants to the mix. This is a Bradley family favourite for dessert, and there are never any leftovers.

Derek & Jimmy's Gingerbread

10 oz flour

3 oz butter

1 teaspoon ground ginger

1 egg

¼ teaspoon ground cinnamon

4 oz dark brown sugar

1 teaspoon salt

¾ teaspoon bicarbonate of soda, dissolved in 3 teaspoons milk

5 oz treacle

Mix the flour, ginger, cinnamon and salt. Melt the treacle and butter over a gentle heat, then leave to cool. Beat the egg and sugar together. Add the melted treacle mix alternately with the beaten egg mix to the flour. Add the dissolved bicarbonate of soda and beat to a soft dropping consistency, adding a little more milk if necessary. Bake in a greased 10 inch square tin in a slow oven for 90 to 120 minutes. Derek says he can keep a piece of this in his pocket for ages, just in case.

Bradley's Right Good Stuffing

4 oz stale breadcrumbs (white or brown)

½ teaspoon ground mace

½ teaspoon dry sage

Pinch dried rosemary

2 oz crushed walnuts

2 oz currants

salt and pepper

Soak the breadcrumbs in hot water, then squeeze as dry as possible. Mix with the currants and seasonings, and use to stuff a pork joint. You can also stuff it into the turkey, or the goose, or the chicken. You can also bake it off on a tray and add it on the side of any meal.

www.ingramcontent.com/pod-product-compliance
Lightning Source LLC
Chambersburg PA
CBHW020915180626
46816CB00007BA/2413